CROOKWOOD

Barbara Elmore

Blue Rose Books

Published by:
Blue Rose Books
4201 Morrow Ave.
Waco, Texas 76710

Library of Congress Catalog Number: 99-068878

ISBN: 0-9676833-1-9

Summary: Angelsea Mead's life seems to fall apart
        the day she suggests her parents get a divorce.

CONTENTS

ONE   Only a Suggestion 1

TWO   A Family Meeting 7

THREE   The Disappearance of Dylan 17

FOUR   A Visit to the New House 23

FIVE   The Big Move 33

SIX   No Visitors Allowed 45

SEVEN   The Invitation 53

EIGHT   A New Friend 61

NINE   The Deal 71

TEN   Visiting With the Doctor 77

ELEVEN   A Rumor Comes and Goes 91

TWELVE   Dylan's Home! 105

THIRTEEN   Once a Monster 115

FOURTEEN   Mom Gets Weird 127

FIFTEEN   The Theft 137

SIXTEEN   Going Shopping 149

SEVENTEEN   Audrette's Surprise 155

EIGHTEEN   A Good Time Was Had 167

NINETEEN   Changes 173

Also by Barbara Elmore

Breathing Room

── ONE ──

Only a Suggestion

Angel should have known better than to try to sneak inside the house, but it was too late now. Her parents' fight had rekindled before she made it to her bedroom and shut the door. She stood in the middle of the room, her hands knotted into fists, as she listened without intending to.

They were in the kitchen on the other end of the rambling house, but she could hear them clearly even with the door closed. This fight was about one of her father's business parties that her mother didn't want to attend. But they'd fight about the weather or the length of the grass if there weren't something else.

Angel hurriedly picked up her book bag and headed for the door, hoping she'd get outside to the patio. Outside you couldn't hear them, and maybe by the time she got her homework done, the argument would be over.

She glanced out the window. There was Dylan walking up San Antonio Street, making his way toward the front door. She didn't want him to hear the arguing. She was in the kitchen before she even knew what she intended to do. Her parents immediately turned toward her, their faces pinched and red.

"What is it?" her mother snapped.

Angel didn't know what to say. The silence became heavy. When her mouth actually opened and words came out, they startled her as much as anyone. She had thought them a million times but never dared utter them. But out they came, and the flow was as unstoppable as a cresting river.

"Since you two don't like each other, why don't you just get a divorce? Because Dylan and I are sick of your yelling."

As soon as the words were out, she wanted to recall them. She studied her mother's white face and widened eyes. Gaylon Mead was breathing so softly you couldn't hear it. Her hands were twisting a cuptowel into a small rope.

Angel turned to look at her father, Gary. As her eyes met his, he looked at the floor. She knew instantly that she had spoken his thoughts. Divorce. The voice in her head told her she was stupid to be surprised. She should leave, but she couldn't. And not only could she not recall her words, she could not keep more from coming.

"Dylan goes to bed with a pillow over his head. Have you ever seen him do that? It makes me sick to

CROOKWOOD

my stomach. You know what I do so I can't hear you?
I wear my headphones and turn the volume way up.
But I can still hear you in my head."

She felt the panic rising in her throat. What was
she going to do now, and why hadn't she thought
about that before? She had always been good at
planning her next move. But this time she hadn't even
thought about it.

Her mother moved toward her with her arm
extended, a pleading look on her face. Angel
involuntarily took a step backward. She turned and
ran out of the kitchen, colliding hard with someone in
the hall. The sweaty smell of her nine-year-old brother
filled her nostrils.

Dylan's bushy brown eyebrows made two perfect
arches. Angel stared at them to avoid his eyes. She
hadn't realized he was already inside the house. He
must have heard enough of what she said to get the
gist of it, and probably felt he had been betrayed. They
had an unspoken pact never to mention the fights.
She pushed past him and ran down the hall and
outside. The sun had gone down and the dimness of
twilight cast soft reflections on the swimming pool in
the back yard. Without stopping, Angel flung her book
bag on the patio table and ran into the garage. She
jumped on her bicycle and pedaled down San Antonio
Street.

When she got the bike for Christmas a year ago,
she thought she'd never use it. Her best friend Cat

didn't have one. Dylan was the only person she knew who ever rode a bike. One day he challenged her to a race. She let him win to get rid of him, then pedaled off on her own. Ever since, she had enjoyed her rare bike rides. She loved the feel of wind in her hair and the zipping sound the tires made on the pavement. She was especially fond of the cover that nighttime provided. She enjoyed slipping by the neighborhood walkers and imagined how they must see her — a mystery girl with her dark braided hair flying straight behind her, visible for only a moment before blending with the darkness.

Usually she could ride her bike until her only reality was tires on asphalt, but not this time. The more she tried not to think about what she'd done, the less she was able to think about anything else. Why hadn't she controlled herself? She didn't want her parents to divorce.

She rode more than an hour before she grew tired, and she turned the bike around and pedaled for home. Her legs felt heavy, as if they were pushing cement blocks. As she coasted into the driveway, two arms reached out of the night and grabbed her handlebars, stopping the bike with a jerk. The hair on Angel's arms stood up until she recognized her mother's perfume.

"Where have you been?" Gaylon demanded. "You left almost two hours ago. I have been worried sick. You know you're not supposed to ride your bicycle after dark!"

She sounded angry, but Angel, peering at her mother's face in the darkness, saw mostly worry lines.

"Where's Dad?" she asked tonelessly.

"He went to a party. Where have you been?" she repeated.

"Nowhere and everywhere. Don't worry — the perverts are at their monthly meeting tonight. No one's prowling for fifteen-year-olds except their mothers. Anyway, what are you going to do when I'm eighteen and free?"

"You'll never be free from me. I'm your mother. Listen, Angel," Gaylon said, her voice becoming serious, "...your father and I — we..."

"Let's just forget it!" snapped Angel, wheeling her bike into the open garage door.

Her mom didn't try to talk again about what had happened, even though Angel wished she would and tried to will her to. Just as she didn't want her parents to divorce, she didn't really want her mother to forget the discussion they were supposed to have about how she was sorry about the fight and how they would try to do better.

But her attempts at willing things to happen had never worked well, and this time was no exception. The house was silent all night, except for the icemaker dumping its cargo and the sizzling of the water heater after Angel took her shower. She thought about knocking on Dylan's door, but there was no sliver of light shining beneath it. He must have gone to bed early.

She sighed and went to her own room. But sleep passed her by until the wee hours of the morning, and then she had a panic-filled dream about being caught with Dylan in the lake in a tiny sailboat during a thunderstorm.

She remembered the dream vividly when her alarm buzzed at six-thirty, and she sat up, startled. Her heart was pounding and she was drenched, but with sweat instead of lake water. She had only been in a sailboat once in her life and didn't have the first idea about how to make it work, especially in a storm. She took the memory as her punishment.

— TWO —

A FAMILY MEETING

The house was quiet when Angel walked home from Cat's and let herself into the back door. She didn't want to see or talk to anyone and headed straight for her room.

"Honey — Angel — is that you? Can you come to the family room?" Gaylon called.

She stood in the hall and considered pretending she hadn't heard. Maybe her mother would give up.

"Angel?"

She sighed and trudged down the hall. As she turned the corner and saw them, she was immediately on guard. Both parents were there, sitting across from each other. No one ever used this room, least of all them.

Her mother smiled one of her too-bright smiles, reserved for strangers, awkward situations, and people she didn't like. "Could you go get Dylan? Your father and I want to talk to you both."

Angel pondered what would happen if she said no. She could say she was sick. Or that she had homework to do. She started thinking of excuses — she should bring in her plants, in case the temperature dipped below freezing. She didn't want the bougainvillea that she had gotten last spring to croak. It was one of her first experiments at successfully growing a plant, and it was big and glorious.

"Angel? Could you do that for me please — get Dylan?" her mother repeated.

Unless she literally ran away, she wasn't going to get out of this. She stalked back down the hall to her brother's room, dreading what she'd find. He'd been weird for a couple of weeks, ever since D-day, which was the label she privately put on her stupid foray into her parents' fight. His weirdness didn't exactly stand out in this family of weirdos, but Angel had noticed. He was quiet almost all the time, and Dylan was never quiet. She couldn't remember the last time he'd been out with his friends. And he'd rejected two of her own invitations to shoot hoops.

She stuck her head inside his room. Books were spread out on his desk and the cursor was blinking on his computer, but he wasn't sitting in front of it. She went in. He was upright on the bed, basketball on his lap, staring at the window. Not out of it, just at it.

"Dill?" He turned to look at her.

"Mom and Dad want us. In the family room." She tried to make her voice sound normal.

"All right."

She kept talking as if he had asked why. "I don't know what's up. Something important, I guess. Maybe they want to announce they're in a midlife crisis."

The Meads were both thirty-four. Gaylon and Gary Mead had married in college and had lived for awhile in a rambling house with a bunch of other students.

Angel had looked through their old photos and tried to imagine what their life was like. She barely recognized her parents from the pictures, her father with a bushy beard and long hair, in contrast to his 90s-style bare face and razor-cut. He was a lawyer, and took "looking the part" very seriously.

And had her mother even known what lipstick was? In all the pictures, her serious face was bare and pale, and her straight hair was long and parted in the middle and decorated with a beaded string tied around her forehead. Her dresses were shapeless and touched her ankles. Angel looked at the big dresses and and wondered if her mother was pregnant with her at the time. There was no year on the back.

Right before Angel was born, Gaylon, then nineteen, postponed college. Gary started going only part time, because he had to get a job. Then, much later, after they both had finished, Dylan came along — their "planned" baby, Gaylon called him. "You were our beautiful surprise," her mother hastened to add, as if Angel's feelings would be hurt because she wasn't part of the plan.

Angel didn't look at the pictures much any more, but she remembered them, and wondered when her parents had stopped liking each other.

The atmosphere in the family room felt like a gathering of wary talk-show guests. Gaylon and Gary sat unmoving, staring into air like gargoyles, and Gaylon was still smiling the fake smile. She patted the sofa beside her and looked at her daughter. "Sit down here." Angel obeyed, heart heavy.

Across from them, a round lacquered coffee table between them, sat her father in his wing chair. Dylan chose the other end of the sofa, away from everyone. He clutched his basketball like a life preserver. Her mother looked at her father and nodded, as if to say the time had arrived.

"Well Angel, Dylan," began Gary, "your mother and I have something to tell you, something not entirely..." His voice faded. He turned his eyes to the floor and shook his head.

"Oh, good grief," Gaylon muttered. "You're the big creator of phrases, the one who knows what to say for any occasion!" Her face was dark with anger or disgust — it was impossible to tell which. Angel's heart began thumping and she felt suddenly alert, poised to leave quickly if shouting began.

But Gaylon didn't yell. She paused and looked at the floor herself, as if there were a list of answers there. Then she looked at Angel and began talking in a calm voice.

"Angel," she began, "when you came into the kitchen the other evening, when your father and I were...talking...do you remember asking us to stop?"

Angel nodded even though her brain rejected the word "talking." Her stomach churned angrily.

"Well, that was a good thing, what you did. It helped us decide to do some things."

Angel's heart raced even faster. If she had done a good thing, why was she so afraid? The urge to leave the room was overwhelming. As she watched her mother rub the palms of her hands together, she gripped the edges of the sofa cushion to make herself stay put. She imagined her hands lashed to the cushion and the cushion to the sofa.

"When we started talking about what we wanted from life, we realized—" her mother glanced at her father "— we don't want the same things anymore."

Angel couldn't hear anyone breathing. Then her father found his voice.

"Your mother and I have agreed to make some changes. We are going to live apart for awhile."

Oh sure, on that they could agree. Angel put her hand on her chest as if to still her pounding heart. She wanted to look at Dylan but was afraid to, afraid of the accusing look she knew must be on his face. If she had just ignored her parents' "talking" like she had always done, none of this would be happening. They'd all be going their separate ways, but at least they'd be doing it in the same house. There was safety in that predictability.

Everything in the room looked blurry, but Angel held in her tears. She spoke in a voice that sounded too high-pitched. "So, what do you want?"

"What?" her mother asked.

"You said you didn't want the same things. What do you want?"

Her mother chewed on her lip. The shrieks of neighborhood children enjoying the clear evening filled the silence. They were everyday sounds, sounds of people living their lives. They seemed out of place amidst the tension in the Meads' family room.

"I don't want to be a nurse any more. I don't want to live in San Marcos, or in any city. I don't want to fight anymore. I hope, one day soon, to define my life in terms of what I do want. But I don't know how to do that right now."

For a fleeting second, Angel wanted to hug her and say that everything would be all right, like her mother had done so many times for her. But the feeling flew away and was replaced with the sense that she was watching a movie she didn't particularly like in a theater full of strangers. She gripped the sofa cushion again as she looked at the faces around her.

"And I do want to live in San Marcos," said Gary, as Angel's eyes fell on his face. "I don't want to move to the country."

"Well, who does?" Angel blurted.

"I do," Gaylon said.

Angel held her breath. Had she misheard?

"I've found us a place out of town. You and Dylan can still go to school here in town, only you'll have to ride the school bus. You'll still have all your old friends. It will be like the best of both worlds."

Angel moved her head from side to side. Wrinkles formed between her eyebrows. "You don't mean we're moving!"

"That's exactly what I mean," said Gaylon. "To an old house. It needs work, but I like projects. Besides, when I quit my job, I'll have lots more time. And you and Dylan can help me!" She forced a cheerful smile. Angel looked away, but not knowing where to look anymore, she focused on Dylan. He was sitting stiffly upright, like someone had nagged him about his posture. He stared at air. The basketball rested in his lap, no longer a life preserver. Angel wondered how much of the conversation he had heard.

She turned back to Gaylon. "I don't get this. Why would we move? If you don't want to live together, why can't Dad move out and leave us here, in our home?"

"No one is staying here," her father said. "We're selling the house. I've found an apartment. It's big enough for you and Dylan to come stay with me if you ever want to."

Angel stared at him, wondering if this could possibly be a bad, bad joke. Payback from her parents, maybe, for meddling. But her parents weren't the type to joke about something like this. Maybe she was asleep and having a bad dream. She pinched her arm until it stung. She was not asleep. This was not a joke and not a bad dream. This was her life.

"I don't understand, Mom. Why can't we stay here?"

"Because I'm quitting my job, Angel. We can't afford this house unless your father and I are both working. I leased the house in Crookwood. It's affordable, and —"

"Crookwood!" exploded Angel, her voice incredulous. "That's thirty miles from town! The only houses out there are crackerboxes or trailer houses, and they're all right on the road!"

"No," said Gaylon, her voice smooth. "It's not a trailer, and it's off the road."

"What are we going to live on if you don't work?"

Her mother looked grim. "When we sell this house, we'll have money. Part of it could be a down payment on a house — maybe on the house we're moving to. But we have to budget carefully. The rest of it is not for you to worry about."

"Hey, I'll be around," said her father.

Angel looked at him. She wanted to say, "No you won't!" but she bit her tongue. She wanted to plug her ears and run. But angry questions, the kind that didn't really need answers, floated in her head.

"Aren't adults supposed to figure out what they want before they have children?" she demanded. "That way you don't mess up everybody's life while you try to figure out where you went wrong."

There was a long silence. Her mother glanced at her father, but he wouldn't look at her.

"Everything can't be about your kids." Gaylon said. "Good things can come from change."

"That's fine for the person who controls the changes!" Angel sputtered. She got up; she had to leave before the tears spilled.

Nobody responded — not that Angel expected anyone to. Her father asked Dylan if he wanted to say anything or ask any questions, and she couldn't remember later if Dylan even shook his head. She knew he didn't speak. He hadn't spoken the whole time.

Angel headed straight for her room, put on her headphones and turned up the volume. Someone knocked on her door once — she sensed it might be her mother — but she didn't answer and whoever it was finally went away. She didn't care if she ever saw anyone in this house ever again. In fact, running away was beginning to look pretty good.

— THREE —

THE
DISAPPEARANCE
OF DYLAN

It was Dylan who ran away. Sort of. Someone who looked like Dylan lived in his room and even wore his clothes, but he wasn't anyone Angel recognized. This Dylan started making D's in school instead of straight-A's. His clothes — the T-shirts and pants that he had carefully chosen himself — began to hang on his shrunken body. And he wouldn't take a bath anymore unless Gaylon insisted.

Dylan had gone somewhere peaceful and sane, and this person was a fill-in. And then the fill-in left, too, several weeks after the session in the family room. The day he disappeared Gaylon met Angel at the door after school. "I have bad news. Dylan's not here." Her words were punctuated by the front door closing. "Your dad and I put him in the hospital today."

The anxiety and anger that had churned inside Angel for days boiled over. She felt her face get hot.

She stomped to her room, throwing her book bag on her bed. Its contents spilled, several books thumping to the floor.

Her mother followed, rubbing her forehead. "I'm sorry, Angel. There was no time to tell you before it happened. We took him to see the doctor this morning, and the doctor referred him to a specialist who said he wanted to admit him right away. Dylan was unresponsive. He just sat there. And the doctor was concerned about his weight loss."

"Guess what, Mom? I've been living here, too! I even remember that Dylan wouldn't come out of his room for school this morning," Angel said, sarcasm drenching her voice. "We don't need a doctor to figure out what's wrong with Dylan. I know exactly what's wrong with him — he feels like he's too much trouble for you to have around. So he tried to be invisible, just like he did when you and Dad fought. Except then he stayed away from home a lot. Lately he's been hiding in his room. And in his head, where it's safe."

Angel's feelings were too strong for her to comprehend. She was angry at herself and at her parents. Now she was angry at Dylan, too. How dare he leave her to face a mess like this alone? She had tried to push away the anger, but it emerged with such force that she couldn't control it. She couldn't explain where it came from or why it was focused on her mother. The best reason was that her mother was there.

The color drained from Gaylon's face. Her hazel eyes grew large. For a moment she didn't speak. She reached out, but Angel shrank away, staring defiantly into her mother's searching eyes. Then Gaylon turned and left.

Angel, who had a headache pounding like a drumbeat, couldn't tell whether Gaylon was stunned or angry or both, and she really didn't care. She slammed the door and flung herself on the bed, staring at the ceiling until finally the pain forced her to close her eyes. When she opened them again, the clock said six a.m. She was on top of the covers, fully dressed.

She sat up. Her headache had subsided and left in its place a thickness, like her head was wrapped in cotton. It was unpleasant, but she'd take it over a headache. She showered and dressed, realizing as she walked to the kitchen and smelled food that she hadn't eaten anything since lunch the day before.

Her mother was cooking, her back to the door. "Good morning," she said, not turning around. "I thought you'd be hungry. I'm fixing eggs, sausage and biscuits. Did you sleep?"

Angel answered with a grunt. She wished she could refuse breakfast, but even the coffee smelled good to her and she didn't drink coffee. She was still angry, and her mother was the only person to be angry at. It made her feel guilty, but the guilt only made her anger worse. It seemed an impossible circle.

She poured herself a cup of coffee as her mother stared, then tried to drink it without making a face. In a few moments, her mother set a plate before her and touched her hair lightly. Ignoring her, Angel tried to eat slowly. She ended up gobbling everything on her plate in less than five minutes then waited for her mother's speech.

There was only silence. Her mother ate a few tiny bites, leaving most of her food on her plate. Then she picked up the dishes and rinsed them. Feeling dismissed, Angel walked to school. She told herself dismally that Dylan's illness would at least postpone, if not end, her parents' plans.

She was wrong about that, too. The red-and-blue "For Sale" sign in the front yard greeted her when she got home. It was as welcome as a slap in the face. All the thoughts she had entertained about having an adult conversation with her mother left her head.

She threw her books on the hall entry table and blew through the house. When she found her mother draining pasta in the steamy kitchen, Hurricane Angel hit with full force. "There's a sign in our yard!" she cried.

Her mother shook the pasta pan over the sink. Clearly, getting every last drop of water out of the noodles was her most important task. "Um-hmm," she said, absently.

"We can't move with Dylan in the hospital," Angel said, trying to keep the desperation out of her voice.

"How can we? He'll be here, and we'll be half an hour away. We should wait until he's out, and then we can decide what to do."

Gaylon looked at her, then spoke distinctly and slowly as if Angel were new to English. "I've already decided what to do, Angelsea. It's too late to turn back now. I've paid for six months on the house in Crookwood, so we need to sell this house as soon as possible. We can't afford both places. And it's not like we're moving to another state. I'll still see Dylan as often as the doctor allows, and so will Gary."

"What about me?

"You can't see him yet. We'll have to wait until the doctor give his approval.

Angel demanded, "What did Dylan say when you told him about all this?"

Her mother's silence told her Dylan didn't know.

"Do you plan on telling him at all?"

"Yes, Miss High and Mighty. As soon as his doctor says I can. You needn't act as if I'm abandoning my son. Go wash your hands. Dinner is in ten minutes. It will just be you and me."

Angel felt like sanity had escaped her, and she picked at her food. When the ordeal of trying to eat was finally over, her mother announced as they cleared the table that it was time Angel saw the Crookwood house.

"I had intended for you and Dylan to see it together, but...you need to see it as soon as possible. We'll go Saturday."

"What's the hurry? We still live here. No one's bought it yet."

Gaylon looked guilty. "The Realtor called while you were changing your clothes. We've had an offer and it's not bad."

Angel looked at her mother in disbelief.

"A young couple went through the house this afternoon, before you got home. They've offered us what we asked for. The catch is, they want us out by the end of the month — two weeks."

Suddenly dizzy, Angel plopped into a kitchen chair. She felt like she was on a merry-go-round that was moving too fast.

Her mother was talking, but she couldn't understand the words. It was just background noise to the roaring in her ears. She put her head down on the kitchen table and closed her eyes.

"Angel, are you all right?" she heard her mother ask.

She stayed at the kitchen table, unmoving, for some time. She was afraid to move and even more afraid to think for fear she'd be sent to join Dylan.

— FOUR —

A VISIT
TO THE NEW HOUSE

"Angel, it's time."

Her mother's voice was soft, a little bit like music. Another time, even three weeks ago, Angel would have liked hearing it. It beat the buzz of her alarm clock. But not today.

She squinted into the dark around her, trying to see daylight behind the mini-blinds. She couldn't make out the numbers on her clock.

"What time is it?" she growled, her voice thick.

But her mother had already gone, flitting here and there and who knew where? Angel had never thought of her as a flitter before. When her mother worked at the hospital, moving so quickly from place to place would have been more appropriate. Now that she didn't work there anymore, she ought to have more time. But she acted as if time were even more precious now, and she refused to stay in one place long.

Angel stayed a minute more in bed, trying not to think about why she had to get up before daylight on a Saturday. But she couldn't keep the thoughts at bay. They had occupied almost every waking moment. Today they were going to see the house in Crookwood. Or she was. She doubted her father would go, as had become the norm lately. Everything was on her shoulders.

"Are you up, Angel?" her mother called. "Breakfast in ten minutes."

"Don't push it," Angel muttered, propelling herself upright.

She dressed without turning on the light, pulling on wrinkled jeans from her closet floor and a faded purple sweatshirt she found in her bottom dresser drawer. She shoved her bare feet into old loafers.

She blinked as she walked into the kitchen, surprised for an instant that her mom was wearing jeans. Then she remembered again that her mom didn't work anymore.

"Where's Dad?" she asked in a monotone.

"He went to look for furniture for his apartment."

"Before daylight? What's open at this hour?"

Her mother didn't answer.

Angel knew he hadn't wanted to be home. He was probably drinking coffee at some greasy cafe that smelled of old scrambled eggs. She wished she were with him. She plopped down at the table and stared at the salt-and-pepper shakers.

Her mother tried to change the subject. "What did Catherine say when you told her you were moving?"

"Not much."

Angel had let the realtor's sign tell Cat about their moving. Cat had reacted the way Angel expected.

"Is the sign in front of your house a joke?" she had asked.

"No joke."

"When were you planning on telling me?"

"I didn't feel like talking about it. My parents are splitting up."

She had debated about telling Cat that last part, but in the end it hadn't mattered. Their conversations had been strained for a month, ever since Cat said Angel should ask her parents for a car, and Angel said no, it wasn't the right time. Not that it ever would be.

Cat barely paid attention to anyone's parents splitting up. Her mother had been married three times, so Angel's parents separating was not a big event to her.

"You haven't told Catherine, have you?" asked her mother.

"I told her you were selling the house. She doesn't know about Crookwood."

"You want dry cereal or oatmeal?" Her mother was trying to change the subject again. Flit, flit.

"Neither." Angel headed for the toaster.

"Today," Gaylon announced, "you will decide which bedroom will be yours. I expect you and Dylan both will want rooms on the second floor. But there is room in the basement, if someone wanted to be down there."

A sudden relief flooded Angel. She had worried that the house would be one of the tiny roadside shoeboxes she pictured every time she thought of Crookwood. If it had a basement, it must be big. And old. Few homes in Texas had basements, as far as she knew.

"Wouldn't a basement be damp and mossy and full of bugs and stuff?" Angel asked. She shuddered. "Dill can have the basement. Too bad he isn't here to decide for himself. Are we just supposed to pick a room for him and hope he likes it?"

Angel couldn't tell if her mother had thought about this, but she didn't seem surprised by the question.

"Yes, I think that would be wise, to have a room ready for him when he gets out of the hospital. Which room to choose is not anything he's thinking about right now. Dylan seems...far removed from day-to-day life. I'm glad you're OK, Angel. No complaints, please. That will help me — help all of us."

Gaylon left to finish getting dressed. "Clean up the kitchen, OK?" she called over her shoulder.

Angel's toast had gotten cold, and the few bites she ate felt like chunks of clay when they went down. As she tossed the rest in the garbage and carried the dishes to the sink, she wondered what was left for her mother to do to get ready. Jeans and a sweatshirt seemed like the right dress code for Crookwood.

She watched her hands as the water ran over them. One of her classmates lived on a dairy farm outside San Marcos. Angel had noticed that her hands were always red and chapped and her cuticles were ragged.

When she finished the dishes, she grabbed the hand cream on the counter and began rubbing blobs of it into the skin around her fingernails. Suddenly, a picture of Dylan hugging his basketball flashed in her head, and she felt guilty for thinking about ragged cuticles.

They left a few minutes later, both of them silent as the car headed further and further out of town. Finally, Gaylon spoke.

"Your bedroom in the new house will be much bigger than the one you have now," she said to Angel. I don't know which room you will choose, but they're all very large. Just remember, when you see them, that none of the bedrooms are in the shape I want them to be in."

Angel knew her mother was waiting for questions, so she refused to ask any.

"Anyway, when your rooms are fixed up, I think they'll be nicer than the ones you have now." She paused. "When they're fixed up," she repeated. "I hope you aren't put off by the condition of the house. It needs work. But I promise it will be beautiful."

"The house we live in now is beautiful," Angel said, twirling the ring she always wore. It had been a present from her parents for making good grades. She guessed there would be no more presents like that in her future.

"Too late to turn back, Angel. Even if we wanted to."

After driving forever over awful roads, Gaylon turned the station wagon off the main road into a lane that Angel would never have noticed. "The county hasn't graded this road in awhile, so it's bumpy," said Gaylon.

"I'll grade it right now," Angel replied. "I give it an F. Better save some money for tires."

She wasn't prepared to see the house when it appeared as if out of nowhere at the end of a circular drive. It sat behind a sidewalk covered with leaves and weeds. Staring at the two-story in front of her, Angel was reminded of a house near the school that the city had torn down because it was leaning.

This house was straight, but it was a dingy gray, any paint that might have brightened it long gone. Two faded green shutters hung lopsided on the second story, framing a broken window. Angel wondered if her mother had lost her mind.

"It'll look better with paint," Gaylon said.

Angel struggled to find something good to say. She spotted a large dandelion rooted in the middle of the cracked front sidewalk. Muddy-green and a good two feet tall, it claimed the property as its own. "I guess the dirt out here is fertile," she offered.

"Let's go inside," Gaylon said.

"Is it safe? When was the last time anyone lived here?"

"Oh, Angel, loosen up! Where is your sense of adventure?"

"I'm not dressed for adventure! I don't want anything to fall on my head."

"The woman who rented it to us just moved out," her mother said with forced patience. "So yes, it's safe."

"Where'd she move to?" Angel asked, getting out of the car.

"To San Antonio to live with her daughter. She was ninety years old and didn't want to live out here by herself anymore."

"You think her daughter would take me in, too?" Angel asked.

"The inside is charming," her mother said, pretending deafness as she opened the door and stepped aside to let Angel pass.

The wood floor was bare, with lighter ovals here and there revealing where rugs had rested. A good cleaning and several dozen coats of wax might help. The wallpaper was stained in some places, falling off in others. The stale odor of mildew hung in the unmoving air. Old drapes contributed to the smell and made the rooms dark.

"What do you think so far? Can you see the possibilities?" her mother asked. "Come on, Angel. I want you to see your bedroom. I mean, if you want it to be."

Angel followed so closely up the stairs that she stepped on the heels of Gaylon's shoes. Her mother turned around, frowning. "Why are you on top of me? Are you scared?"

"Of course not!" lied Angel. She found the house spooky.

The room her mother had chosen for her was huge, big enough for a four-poster. Big enough for a grand piano, or even a small bowling alley. Angel liked the size. Then her mother pointed out the bathroom down the hall.

"No connecting bathroom?" she wailed.

"You'll still have to share with Dylan," her mother said.

"In a house this big? I can't believe a house so huge wouldn't have a bathroom for every bedroom!" Her mother flitted away.

Alone in her new room, Angel walked to a huge window and looked out. The view of rolling hills, smudged with browns and greens, surprised her. She hadn't expected anything so pretty.

Tearing herself from the view, she turned and studied the room. A picture of the carpeted, blue bedroom and tiled bath she'd left an hour ago appeared in her head. She squeezed her eyes shut to erase that scene, opened them again and tried to imagine this room as it could be. With new wallpaper and paint, it might be all right. She had never painted or papered a house, but her mother had. She Who Had Done Everything, Angel called her secretly. Everything but live in the country, which was her "dream". When Angel asked her mother how long she had been dreaming of the country life, Gaylon wouldn't answer. Why couldn't living on a beach in California have been her dream?

As she wandered through the house, seeing how big it was, she imagined Gaylon and herself as two lone ants, moving about a big mound. Were there enough of them to survive the work ahead?

She ached with loneliness for the rest of her family. Especially for Dylan. If he were here, at least they could make jokes that only they would understand. That would get them both through the trauma. Now they had to go through separate traumas separately.

She wondered if he'd ever be well enough to live in Crookwood. Or even for her to visit. She felt guilty for thinking of her measly problem as a trauma. And guiltier when she realized that she had caused this mess to begin with.

— FIVE —

THE BIG MOVE

The offer on the Meads' house came two days later, and moving day was only a weekend away. At night, Angel helped her mother box up pots and pans, dishes and towels, knick-knacks and books. She avoided packing her own things until the last minute in case the plan changed.

When it was finally time to move, she had only a couple of hours to pack. In a panic she tossed her clothes into cardboard boxes and two ugly black suitcases that her father had given her. She didn't fold anything, but kept her hands moving as if she were an assembly line worker—grab dress, take off hanger, toss in box. Once through with the closet, she moved to her chest of drawers. She didn't stop until everything was in a box or a suitcase. Everything except a plaque hanging on her wall, which she had decided to leave behind.

Not until she went to the kitchen for a drink did her world cave in. Her father was loading his suitcases into his car. Angel stood motionless, water bottle suspended, the thought of separation slamming into her like a truck. She didn't know when she'd see her father again. Tonight she'd try to sleep in a strange room, and if she called out, her mother would be the only one there.

She dropped her bottle of water and fled the kitchen. She had to escape but didn't know where. She ended up in the garage looking at dead plants. No one had remembered to bring them in the night the balmy weather in San Marcos was pushed out by a bitter norther and the temperatures suddenly plunged below freezing. Her anger built as she stared at the plants, all of them black, withered, and unrecognizable. Grabbing what she thought was a dead geranium, she carried it to the dented metal garbage can. "This is for Cat!" she cried, raising the clay pot above her head and letting it go.

Cat had shrugged when Angel told her she was moving to Crookwood. "I'll have to get someone else to help me with my homework, I guess," she'd said. "But I'd sure like to know where I'm going to go swimming now."

She hadn't bothered to come by today, as she had promised. Hearing the clanking, crunching sound as it hit bottom gave Angel a perverse satisfaction.

She moved on, dedicating each dead plant to someone before dropping it—Gary, Gaylon, Beth Ann, Rhonda, Harmon. She wasn't actually mad at the last three, who were all Cat's friends, but she didn't like them. They got smaller plants. When she was finished, she stared into the can at the heap of roots, dirt, and pieces of clay pot. A movement in the doorway caught her eye, and she looked up to see her father. She wondered how long he had been there but she didn't ask.

"They're all dead," she said weakly. "Freeze got 'em."

"Can I have this one?" he asked, pointing at one she had missed, a bare-limbed bougainvillea. Just a few weeks ago, it was bushy and blooming, basking in the mild January weather. Now it was a twig with thorns.

"I don't care!" Angel snapped, brushing past him into the house. She stomped to her room. The movers, who had been waiting earlier for her to finish packing, had swooped in and taken everything. That made her even angrier. She plopped down in the middle of the floor and glared at the lacquered wooden plaque on the wall, titled "Angelsea." She'd let the new owners of the room throw it away.

Angelsea was her full name. The Meads had named her after a song by Cat Stevens, whose records and tapes they had once collected. Before she was two months old, her parents had glued and varnished the lyrics to "Angelsea" onto the plaque, which they hung in her room. It had hung in four different bedrooms and was in surprisingly good shape despite being carried all over town. Angel had dusted it every week since she was old enough to take care of it.

"Aren't you taking that with you?" Her father had come in so quietly that she jumped.

"Are you following me?" She looked at him. "Anyway, why move it every time, like it's something special?"

He sat down on the floor beside her. "It is special. I can remember the day Gaylon and I made it. You were only about a month old. Did you know we chose your name as soon as your mom found out she was pregnant?"

Angel snorted. "I suppose you would have named a boy Angelsea, too!"

"Oh, your mom knew you were a girl. When she told me, we both said 'Angelsea' at the same time. And I cut out the wood for the plaque right away. We had a friend who knew how to do calligraphy, and she copied the words. That plaque was probably the first thing we ever hung on the wall."

Angel felt a hard knot in her stomach. She wanted to hit the plaque against something until it broke.

"I don't want it anymore. I don't like it and it doesn't match my room at Crookwood." That was absurd. Nothing and everything matched her cavernous room at Crookwood. But she wanted her father to feel as badly as she did.

"All right," he said, rising easily and lifting it off

the wall. "I'll take it with me, then. When you want it back, you let me know."

"When you want us back, let me know!"

"So that's what you think." Her father stood motionless, the plaque in his hand. "That's just wrong, Angel. I'm still your father. You're still my family."

"In case you hadn't noticed, we're going to be living with Mom. So you leaving her means you're leaving me, too."

"But you can come to my apartment anytime. I mean that. We can even have a regular time for you to come every week, if you want. Gaylon and I will do whatever it takes."

"Except live together like a real family." When she said it, her voice choked. She'd told herself she wasn't going to cry today. She had done enough of that. But she felt her nose stinging and the tears welling up in her eyes, and she couldn't stop them from spilling down her cheeks. "How is visiting you the same? You know it isn't!"

Her father knelt down in front of her and put his arms around her. She didn't have the energy to move even if she'd wanted to. They stayed there like that for a long time, with her crying silently. Although she felt miserable, she didn't want the moment to end because when it did he'd be gone.

Too soon, he kissed the top of her head. "I know it isn't the same," he whispered. "But it'll have to do."

Then he got up quickly, walking away so lightly Angel didn't hear him leave. She remained on the floor awhile longer, brushing away tears. She no longer felt angry. Just weary.

"Angel! You ready?" her mother called. "Can you bring your stuff?"

She rose and picked up a suitcase and a box, struggling out the door. She trudged to her mother's station wagon and handed them to her to load. Her mother always packed the car, no matter where they were going. She was precise and organized, and could pack more into a car than anyone else. She was too busy to look at Angel, so she didn't see the red eyes and nose. "You just threw your clothes in boxes?" her mother asked. "They're going to be all wrinkled."

Angel didn't feel like answering. She noticed that Dylan's bags were already loaded and wondered who had packed them. She stared at the three red nylon bags, dingy and tattered. Dylan had gotten them for Christmas when he was six. He had been so proud of them that he packed as many of his clothes as he could cram inside. He had literally dressed out of the bags every morning until Gaylon had gotten tired of seeing wrinkled shirts and had made him unpack it all.

"What bags did Dylan take to the hospital?" Angel asked, suddenly concerned he didn't have his red bags.

"No bags," said Gaylon. We just take him clothes as he needs them. Go get the rest of your things. We need to get to Crookwood before dark."

The sight of Dylan's bags made her sad. She turned away, went inside and brought out everything else. When they were finished, she and her mother made a last-minute check inside and left together. About halfway down the front walk, they turned in unison to look at what had been their home.

The "For Sale" sign was gone, the leaves raked and the front walk swept clean. They'd cleaned the pool last week, and everything inside was spotless except for a small grape juice stain on the gray-blue carpet in Dylan's room. "Hope they're happy here," said her mother, turning and heading for the car.

Angel lingered a moment more, focusing on the stained glass panel in the front door. She remembered the day they had moved in, and how impressed she'd been with the glass. She had peered through it, trying to see in, but couldn't. And the pool and lush garden in the back yard were like what she imagined paradise to be. She and Dylan had been so excited to get a house with a pool.

She got in the car. She closed her eyes tightly as her mother steered the station wagon away. When the house was far in the distance, Angel glanced at her mother. Gaylon's face was composed, as if she was thinking about something. She didn't look sad at all. Angel hadn't expected her to cry because she hardly ever did, but this was too much; her mother looked as if she was driving to the mall.

"You don't regret leaving at all, do you?" Angel asked.

"I told you—we can't turn back."

She was always looking ahead, planning for the future. She was practical at the worst times, and for some reason that irritated Angel the most.

Angel gritted her teeth and looked straight ahead, too. She wasn't going to cry anymore. She would treat this as just another day in her life. No big deal.

The movers had a key to the Crookwood house and Gaylon's drawing of where to put the furniture, so they were already at work when the Meads arrived. The house looked a little better with their furniture, but the work that faced them made Angel feel tired. "I don't see how you can look forward," she grumbled. "There's too much to do here. Our other house we just moved into—we didn't have to do anything to it."

Her mother rubbed her hands together. She looked excited and happy, which Angel couldn't understand. "So—let's get to work," she said.

Angel shook her head and headed upstairs to her room, newly painted and papered on one wall. It had taken her and her mother four afternoons after school, but Angel had been surprised at how easy it was to change the looks of it. She had had fun, too, but wouldn't admit it.

The results were a success because of her mother's ideas. The wall behind the bed was now a garden of tiny pink, purple and yellow flowers. The other three walls and the ceiling were pale yellow, candlelight. Angel had decided on the paper and paint herself, and had suggested papering only one wall. She had picked out the paper with that in mind. On four walls, the flowers would look fussy. On one wall, they looked just right.

Three walls of the room were full of windows, two on each wall. She and her mother had hung off-white pleated shades. Her mother had gasped at the price, but gave in because Angel hadn't wanted curtains. She was hanging her wrinkled clothes in the huge closet when she heard a phone ring downstairs. It sounded far away. "Angel, it's for you," her mother called after a moment. "It's Catherine."

Forgetting her anger, Angel almost fell down the stairs in her haste. "Hello?" she yelled to be heard over the shouts of the movers and her mother. She wished she had her own phone like she did in town. But her mother said they could afford only one phone.

"Angel? Did I miss saying goodbye? You guys sure left early! Listen, can you go shopping next Saturday? A bunch of us are driving to Austin in Harmon's new car."

Angel wondered how Harmon had gotten a car. Out-of-town trips were a luxury for all of them, and until now, no one had owned a car.

"I don't know, Cat." Getting into town would be a problem, but she didn't want to bring it up.

"I need to know for sure right away. Harmon might want to ask someone else."

"I doubt I can go, Cat. I just don't have the money, with the move and Dylan in the hospital. Mom's not working any more, either."

She added the last part because she was embarrassed at blurting out Dylan's situation. She hadn't told anyone about that. But if Cat heard it, she gave no indication. She babbled something about seeing Angel later, then hung up.

"What did Catherine want?" asked her mother.

"She's planning a shopping day in Austin and wanted to know if I could go."

"Uh huh. Are you going?"

"I told her I couldn't afford it."

Her mother chewed her lip. "I'm sorry about the money thing, Angel. But since I'm not working, our budget's going to be tight. We'll have what we need, but I'm afraid I can't give you money for shopping like I used to."

"So I'll just be stuck out here? No shopping at all? How am I supposed to pay for stuff?"

"You'll get a small allowance, and you'll have to live within it, except for necessities. I'll pay for them."

"What about clothes?"

"You have gobs of clothes."

The movers called her, almost as if she had timed it that way, and she left, the relief obvious on her face.

Angel was left alone in her room, with the cheerful pink and purple flowers in the wallpaper mocking her. She threw a shoe at the wall, tearing a tiny hole in the paper right above the bed. That made her feel better.

—— SIX ——

No Visitors Allowed

Activity kept loneliness at bay, Angel reasoned, so she kept busy. During school, she moved from class to class and wrote down every word her teachers spoke. At home, she painted walls, scrubbed windows, and hung pictures.

Nothing could fill up all her hours, though. She still ate by herself at school, finding out-of-the-way places so no one would see her eating sandwiches brought from home. It was during those times when thoughts of Cat and the others, eating lunch in the Lair, crept into her head, uninvited. The Meads didn't have money for the Lair these days.

During class, the ones she and Cat had at the same time, she felt like a blinking neon sign as she sat alone in her regular spot near the middle of the room, while Cat made it a point to sit elsewhere. Cat avoided her so pointedly that Angel went into the bathroom to check for zits and blew on her hand to see if she had bad breath.

At home, she had to stop herself from yelling for Dylan when she walked through the door. They used to shoot hoops in the back yard when the weather was nice. She constantly caught herself checking for him on the school bus, and at least once a day she went by his room at home before remembering that he wouldn't be there.

But the daytime loneliness and insecurity weren't the worst. That came at night, when she tried to sleep in the cavernous old house. Even when she squeezed her eyes shut, her mind never stopped. It was too busy with thoughts of what Dylan was doing, and how it was her fault he was at Childrens Hospital in San Marcos instead of with them.

Did they lock Dylan's room at night? Were there rails on his bed to keep him from falling out? Was he still a zombie, like he was right before he went into the hospital, or was he more like the old Dylan now? Did they give him drugs?

One particularly bad night the thoughts rolled round and round in her head until well after one a.m. Angel finally drifted off after promising herself that she would see Dylan the next day. She hadn't seen him since he'd gone into the hospital weeks before, even though she asked her mother several times a week if she could visit. Each time, Gaylon just shook her head and said not yet.

The next day, she skipped lunch and used the phone in the office at school to call the hospital. When she got through to the right area, she asked when visiting hours were. The woman hesitated before responding, "The patient's doctor should have told you when you could visit. Visits are structured here."

"He did, but I forgot."

"Who is the patient?"

"I'd rather not say."

"You need to make an appointment so we will know you're coming."

Angel thanked her and hung up. She knew she'd never see Dylan this way. She decided to just show up at the hospital. Surely they wouldn't send her away. She would cut her last class, phys ed, and walk. If she hurried, she could get there in twenty minutes. She could visit Dill for a little while before heading back to school to catch the bus.

But she miscalculated the time. The hospital was thirty minutes away, even walking fast. And she hadn't counted on more obstacles at the hospital. Precious minutes ticked away while she hunted for the correct door. Finally, she saw a small sign that said "Entrance" on a door that didn't face the street. She pulled the handle, but the door was locked. Then she spotted a button to the right of the door and pressed it. In a moment a young woman dressed in street clothes came to the door, looked at Angel for a moment, then peered behind her to see if she was alone. "Yes?" she said through the crack in the door.

"I'm here to visit my brother, Dylan Mead."

The woman stared at her for a moment, then took a clipboard hanging by the door and began leafing through the pages. After a moment, she shook her head. "Dylan Mead is not on my list of patients who can have visitors. And we don't have any visitor appointments scheduled this afternoon."

"I'd have to be on a list? Why? I'm his sister."

"That's something you would need to ask his doctor."

Angel stared at the woman, from her red hair which fell in waves to her shoulders to her green eyes, to her button lips, outlined in brown and filled in with a mauve tint. Her blue badge, which stood out against the dark green of her suit jacket, bore the name Lindy Droza.

"Ms. Droza, could I speak with Dylan's doctor, then? I'd like to ask when I could see my brother."

The woman's face softened as she smiled. "I hate to keep telling you no, but that isn't possible, either. The doctor isn't here. He comes only at certain times of the day." She paused and looked down as a beeper went off. She pushed back her jacket to reveal the small black gadget attached to her waistband and peered at it for a moment before telling Angel she was going to have to go. "Is there anyone I can call to come get you?"

"No, thanks," said Angel, backing away from the door. She turned and walked quickly away, feeling the woman's eyes on her back as she reached the street.

She ran most of the way back to school, but the buses had already left. As she plopped down on the curb to figure out where the nearest phone was, she realized that her books were locked inside the school. She took a deep breath and wrinkled her nose at the unpleasant smell of sweat on her clothes. As she tried to lift the braid off the back of her neck, she realized it was half unfastened.

"I am the biggest loser on Earth!" she said aloud. She felt like crying.

Her misery made her oblivious to the cars going by, so she jumped when a voice yelled at her, "Hey! Are you all right?"

She looked up into the tanned face and dark blue eyes of Clifton Neal, a senior whom she'd had a crush on since last year, when he smiled at her in the hall. She crossed her arms tightly, hoping he wouldn't notice that her shirt was wringing wet.

Without waiting for her to answer, he drove his pickup truck up the street, made a U-turn and pulled into the parking lot behind her. He drove as close as possible to where she sat, leaned over to the passenger side and rolled down the window. "Do you need a ride somewhere?"

Angel stared at him wordlessly. She wanted to tell him that she liked his gleaming blue pickup and his crisp white shirt and his beautiful eyes, and that she'd ride anywhere with him. But the words that finally came out of her mouth were "No thanks." She tried to smile, but her mouth was dry so she was sure it looked more like a grimace.

"OK. Later, then." He waved.

She tried to manage a cool look, whatever that was, as she imagined him staring at her in his rearview mirror. She made sure the pickup truck was out of sight before she heaved herself up from the curb. She needed to find a phone.

She'd walked only half a block before she heard a car pull up beside her. Not Clifton Neal again! She was afraid to look.

A familiar voice called her name. She turned around to see her father. She let out her breath in relief. "Come get in the car."

She was too embarrassed even to look at him, and neither of them spoke for a moment. Then her father said, "So you went to see Dylan."

Angel nodded. She had supposed someone would call her parents about Dylan's strange visitor.

"A woman from the hospital called Gaylon," he said. "She was worried about you being out there all alone — she said she didn't see a car or anything. You mind waiting at my office for a little while? I have a couple of things to do, then I'll take you to Crookwood."

"No, I don't mind waiting. Was Mom mad?"

"She didn't sound mad. But sometimes you can't tell," he said.

At least that meant she hadn't been yelling. That was a good sign.

"Dad?" Angel asked. "Do you get to visit Dylan?"

He didn't answer right away as she expected him to. She glanced over at him. His face was sad, and for the first time she noticed there were gray circles under his eyes. "Not unless you'd call fifteen minutes a week a visit," he said.

Angel was stunned. "Is that all?"

Gary nodded. "The doctor said it wasn't good for him to be around his family a lot, not yet anyway. Your mother and I go see him together once a week."

"Next time would you ask the doctor if I could see Dylan? Just for a few minutes?"

"I'll ask. We'll work something out."

For once, Angel was glad that her father's office was dark and boring. No one noticed that she smelled bad and they left her alone as she sat in the corner and paged through a magazine. Plus, her father didn't fake any interest in how her life was, even on the long ride home. He was quiet, lost in thought, just like she was.

She hoped he'd come inside and see how good the house looked and Gaylon, too, for that matter. But he didn't turn the engine off as he pulled up to the front walk and said, "Here we are. Tell your mother hi for me," adding quickly, "I'm not coming in."

He didn't even return her wave as he left, and Angel felt small and drab as she watched the red taillights disappear down the lane.

—— SEVEN ——

THE INVITATION

Angel dreaded her mother's anger and steeled herself for the Inquisition. So she was totally unprepared for Gaylon's complete silence on the matter.

She and Gaylon talked endlessly about everything else, such as which room to tackle next, and what color to paint it. Or what Angel wanted for supper, or whether she could wear her jeans to school one more day before Gaylon washed them.

It was three days after her trek to the hospital before her mother brought it up, and even then she mentioned it indirectly. They were painting what would be the family room, and Angel was working on the baseboards. She had gotten quite good at invisible brush strokes, and she was admiring her work when her mother broached the subject.

"When did you put all of Dylan's things away?" she asked.

"What?"

"Dylan's suitcases. I went in his room to unpack his suitcases the other day, and they were already empty. All of his clothes were hanging up or folded in his chest of drawers. When did you do it?"

"How do you know it was me?" Angel asked. Her mother was silent so long Angel could not resist turning around to look. Gaylon was staring at her with a half-smile on her face. "Maybe it was fairies," said Angel.

"I wish they would paint the house, then."

"You've already got me. Don't be greedy."

Her mother chuckled and was silent a moment. Then she said, "I knew you missed your brother, Angel, but I didn't know how much. I'm sorry you couldn't see him at the hospital."

Angel couldn't answer. She felt an aching loneliness, not only for Dylan, but for her previous life, for her father, for someone to talk to, and she couldn't say that without her voice cracking. So she was silent, and neither of them brought up Dylan again.

She saw Cat at the lockers the next day, the first time in days she had seen her without anyone else around. Angel found herself wondering what to say. She took a deep breath and walked over. "Hi, Cat. I've missed seeing you." She was pleased that the words sounded natural.

"Oh. Hello," Cat said, glancing over the locker door at Angel before going back to what she was doing. Her indifference stung, but Angel decided to let it go.

"How've you been?" she asked, swallowing her irritation. "I haven't talked to you since...in a couple of days."

"Busy. I haven't even seen you at lunch," Cat said. Her tone sounded accusing.

"I've been bringing my lunch and eating outside," Angel replied. "I'm reading 'A Tale of Two Cities'."

"Oh. Why are you bringing your lunch instead of going to the Lair?"

"Money's kind of tight. How was the shopping trip?"

Cat's face brightened. "We had tons of fun! We all got facials and bought new clothes. We're planning on going at least once a month!"

Hoping she was smiling, Angel backed away. "Good," she squeaked. "It's been good talking to you." She returned to her locker and stared inside without seeing, sad about the way her friendship with Cat was ending, jealous of others taking her place. She never expected it to end in the first place, and certainly not like this, a drifting apart with neither of them trying to stop it. Maybe she could still fix it. She whirled around and called to Cat, "Why don't you come out this weekend?"

Cat, clearly surprised, hesitated. "To Crookwood? Why?"

"For the second time, Angel held back her irritation. "Just to hang out. We can hike, or watch TV, whatever you'd like. You can stay over."

"All right. That sounds OK."

It wasn't an enthusiastic endorsement, but it sounded like progress. Angel felt elated.

Later in the week, Cat hedged when Angel asked if she would stay over. If she had let herself think about it, she would have wondered why Cat couldn't give her an answer. But she was too excited to think about such details. They had much to catch up on. Once Cat visited Crookwood and saw it wasn't so bad, Angel was sure she would want to spend the night.

She asked her mother if they could have pizza and garlic bread, Cat's favorites, for dinner. Toward the end of the week she cleaned her room, even under the bed. She examined the entire house, trying to see it through the eyes of a critical visitor like Cat. They had made progress, though there was still much to do. The floors were a warm honey color, the windows sparkled, and the dark drapes were gone, replaced by shades or in some cases, a simple valance. Most of the downstairs had brand-new paint. All the rooms were white, except for the family room, which was pale yellow. Paintings and other items her parents had acquired over the years helped make the place look more like home. It wasn't House Beautiful and it didn't have a pool, but it was interesting. And the only place she had to live. It would have to do.

When Angel phoned the Martin house Saturday morning to doublecheck when Cat would be there, she got Mrs. Martin instead. "Oh, hello, Angelsea. How's life in Crookwood?"

For the first time, Angel didn't cringe at the question. "I'm learning to adjust. I miss Cat, though. Is she there? I wanted to ask her when she was coming."

"She's running errands. May I give her a message?"

"Yes, please. Could you tell her I'm counting on her to spend the night? She should bring her hiking boots. And if you want to drop her off instead of giving her your car for the weekend, my mom and I can bring her home tomorrow."

There was silence for a moment. Then Mrs. Martin said, "I'll ask Cat to call you as soon as she gets back."

Angel waited near the phone almost an hour before deciding that Cat's mother had given her the message and everything was fine. The day was bright and sunny and she didn't want to sit around inside. She ventured outdoors and found her mother in the back yard digging holes on a bare plot of earth. The ground had been covered with winter grass but Gaylon dug it up as soon as they moved in.

She wore a giant straw hat, leather gloves, a dingy white, long-sleeved t-shirt, baggy gray sweatpants and dirty white tennis shoes. The ground was wet from a recent rain, so mud spattered her face, hair and clothes.

Angel couldn't even remember what she'd looked like in nurses' scrubs.

"Did you move out here just so you could go around looking like that?" Angel teased. Gaylon straightened up, untying the kerchief around her neck and mopping her face, which left a smear of mud on her cheek. She took a sip of water from the bottle she always carried with her. Except for the brown smudge, her cheeks were bright pink. "No one who knows you would ever recognize you," Angel continued. "You know we're having company, don't you?"

Her mother grinned. "I'll scrub up. I promise not to wear mud to dinner."

"Or dirt under your fingernails?"

"Can't promise that." She looked around her. "How do you like it?"

Angel had to admit she was surprised by her mother's skill with dirt. She seemed to know intuitively what would grow and where to plant it. Flowers and shrubs native to the area had replaced at least a third of what had been grass, and more grass disappeared every day. Her mother repeated that it made no sense to water something and mow it down.

"We'll appreciate that in the spring and summer," she said.

There was an unconstructed style to her landscaping, allowing for a leisurely stroll among pungent flowers and shrubs. Her mother promised the blooms would attract birds, butterflies and bees in the spring, and she looked forward to making her own dried flower arrangements.

"It's fine," answered Angel, trying not to sound as unenthusiastic as Cat, even thought she felt she had reason. "But why are you doing so much work on a house you don't even own?"

"It's just a garden, Angel. I get inspired watching things grow. Why don't you help?"

"Oh, all right," Angel grumbled. "There's nothing else to do anyway." She found some dingy cotton gloves and a pickaxe, and soon she was digging a two-foot-deep hole, under her mother's instruction, for a small Texas sage bush with silvery leaves.

As she packed soft topsoil around the sage's slim trunk, she sensed her mother was about to say something. She glanced up surreptitiously. Gaylon's forehead was creased in thought. "Angel," she said finally, "maybe you should have other friends over besides Cat."

"What other friends? I don't have any. Cat's been my best friend — my only friend — forever."

"Sometimes you can't plan or predict who your friends will be. Keep an open mind."

"What do you mean?" Angel asked, just as she heard the phone ring. She sprinted up the back steps, catching the phone on its sixth ring. "Hello?" she said breathlessly.

"Angel? It's about time! I thought you weren't going to answer. I was about to hang up!" Cat paused, as if waiting for an apology. Angel was silent, preparing for what was to come next.

"Listen, I can't come out today. Something has come up."

"Like what?"

"Just stuff. You know. Anyway," Cat finished weakly, "maybe we can do this another time. All right?"

Angel hung up without answering. She had known down deep that this was coming, but had chosen to ignore what she knew. She felt stupid. And used.

She turned around and almost ran into her mother, who had come inside quietly.

"Cat can't come."

"I see."

"I'm going to my room for awhile." Her mother nodded and stepped aside to let her pass.

Once in her room with the door shut, Angel stared at her flowered wallpaper and wondered if life could get worse.

—— EIGHT ——

A New Friend

There would be no brooding over Cat. As much as Angel would have loved to play out what might have happened had Cat come over, or fantasize about getting even, there was no thinking about anything else after Gaylon dropped her bombshell. All energies were focused on one thing.

"Angel," Gaylon said the Monday morning soon after Cat's non-visit, do you remember what you said when Dylan went into the hospital?"

Angel nodded. She remembered all too well, although she had tried to blot out her angry words and hoped that her mother had, too.

"You said that he'd withdrawn from the family because he wasn't sure there was a place for him in it any more."

Angel plopped down in a kitchen chair and rubbed her eyes. It was early; she'd just awakened, and all she'd done so far was wash her face, pull on her jeans and shirt, and fix her hair. Getting her bangs to sweep the right direction had been her biggest challenge so far. Besides, she had wanted to talk about important stuff for a long time but her mother had rebuffed all her attempts. So what was so important all of a sudden?

"What you said is similar to something the doctor said," Gaylon continued. "He told us that Dylan felt threatened by the separation, and vulnerable about his position in the family. How did you know that? Is it because that's the way you feel?"

Angel went to the toaster to give the fog time to clear. She took a deep breath, and waited a few seconds to see if her mother would say anything else. The only sound was the clock ticking.

"What does that mean — 'vulnerable about his position in the family'?" Angel asked. "Does it mean that he thinks you're the whole family now, and he worries that one day you won't be here either?"

"I guess that's what it could mean," Gaylon said.

The clock ticked off more seconds. The toast popped up, and Angel took her time buttering it, then carried the plate and a glass of orange juice to the table. She took a deep breath, letting it out slowly.

"I never meant for Dylan to hear what I said to you and Dad that day when you were fighting. The fights always bothered him worse, I think. I hated to hear you yell at each other, too, but lots of my friends have parents who fight. Not that I wanted you guys to be like everyone else, but —" She stopped. She was getting off the subject. "Dylan thought your fights meant you hated each other. And I don't know why, but I think he blamed himself."

"But our fights were never about him! Why would he think that?"

"I don't know why, Mom — I already said that! I don't have an explanation for everything!" snapped Angel, her anger flaring. She glared at her mother, who placed her palms in front of her as if saying "OK."

Angel continued. "Maybe he thought he should've been home more, helped more with chores. And when you think it's your fault, it's pretty easy to think that maybe the whole family will go off and leave you. I know it sounds kind of silly to you, but try to see it from his side." She paused.

"When's Dylan coming home, anyway?"

Her mother shook her head. "The doctor says he doesn't know. There's something else, Angel. He would like for you to come to some of our weekly counseling sessions."

"What weekly counseling sessions?" Angel held a bit of toast, which had been headed for her mouth, in mid-air. She sensed that the bomb was just about to fall.

"Oh, that's right. I haven't told you. Your dad and I meet every Wednesday with Dylan and the doctor, and we talk about things."

"Things? What things? What do you talk about?" Angel asked warily.

"Family life. What caused us to fight. What we thought about our lives and what Dylan thought. It's been enlightening."

"Dylan's actually talking?"

Her mother nodded. Angel shifted in her seat as she tried to see herself sitting in a room while a stranger analyzed her family life. Her parents' fights had been hard enough to bear. Now she was supposed to relive them with a stranger, and say how she felt while they were happening. How humiliating. And then the doctor would get around to what she did, and realize that her parents split up and Dylan got sick right after that. And he would know that she was the cause of everything, that she was the culprit who hadn't done enough to keep her family together

"Great," she said. "The doctor won't let me see Dylan, but he wants to see me? I don't like the rules."

"It might help Dylan. It might help you, too."

"I don't need help!" snapped Angel, her face hot.

"I didn't say you did."

The clock ticked loudly. Angel could hear her heart thumping and wondered if her mother heard it, too.

"Can I think about it?"

"Of course. No one wants to force you to go. The doctor says there's a piece of the puzzle missing without you, that's all."

She left for school hurriedly, thinking she would just as soon let the picture be created without her piece of the puzzle, thank you very much. But the nagging worry that she'd be refusing a chance to help Dylan nibbled at her conscience. If only she had someone she trusted to talk to, someone not connected to her family. It would help just to be able to say, "I'm afraid if I talk to the doctor, everyone will find out my secrets."

She never would have noticed the flyer on the bulletin board in the library if she hadn't been searching for an answer. On the flyer's dark blue background was superimposed the face of a blond girl. "Having problems?" said the caption beneath her serious face. "See your guidance counselor." Beneath that was a note that said the counselor, Mona Bailey, was there Monday, Wednesday and Friday afternoons. And beneath those words someone had scrawled awkwardly, "You'll feel so much better to talk to someone who has worse problems than you do."

Ignoring the comment, Angel considered the possibility. She had heard that Mrs. Bailey was nice, and school counselors were supposed to be trained to help. She thought about it while she chewed on her sandwich at lunch. By the time she got to her apple, she'd made a decision. Right before the warning bell sounded signaling three minutes to get to class, she went to the counselor's office and signed up for a 3:15 p.m. appointment.

She was sorry almost immediately. How pathetic was she? No one went to the counselor. If anyone found out, she would be the butt of every joke until school was over.

At first she thought she would just skip the appointment, but then decided the counselor might try to track her down. So she would keep the appointment, but make up another problem. She arrived in the counselor's office precisely at 3:15.

Mrs. Bailey wore her brown hair in a straight pageboy. Her brown-framed glasses matched her hair, and so did her eyes. Her navy suit, white blouse and low-heeled navy shoes were neat, prim and exactly what Angel expected.

What she hadn't expected was Mona Bailey's wide smile and friendly eyes. Lying to those eyes would not be easy.

"I don't believe I have met you, Angelsea," she said. "Please sit down."

"Thank you," said Angel, plopping down so quickly that she almost missed the chair.

"Let's see, you are a sophomore?" said the counselor, writing in a notebook.

Angel nodded nervously. "And I'm too tall," she blurted. Best to get the lie out in a hurry.

"What?"

"That's why I'm here. I'm too tall for my age. Boys don't like me because I'm so tall. Neither do the girls.

They don't trust me. I don't have any friends." At least that was true.

Mrs. Bailey stopped, pen hovering in mid-air. She considered Angel, looking only at her eyes, then glanced down at her notes. After a moment, she cleared her throat. "Has this been a longtime problem for you, or is it one that just occurred?"

Angel realized she had not given this enough thought. She'd have to keep making things up. "For about, let's see, several years."

"I see. How tall are you?"

"Five-six. No. Five-seven." She shrugged. "I lose track." She looked pointedly at Mrs. Bailey's hands. The counselor wasn't taking notes any longer. She wasn't doing anything but staring at Angel, who shifted in her seat.

"Being too tall isn't really a problem for you, is it, Angelsea?" she said gently, after a few moments.

"No," said Angel, shifting her stare to her own hands.

"Would you like to come back some other time, maybe?"

Angel nodded miserably and got up. She had only made things worse by coming here and telling a lie. To her surprise, the counselor said, "Try not to feel bad. This happens a lot. But do try to find someone you can talk to."

"Thanks for not being mad," she said, and hurried away to catch the bus. She plopped down in the first open seat she saw, barely noticing the person next to her. She studied her shoes, and the floor.

Suddenly, a magazine picture of a girl with a toothy smile and a shiny wedge-cut was thrust into her lap. "You could wear your hair like this," said the voice next to her. "It's a classic and would fit your features. I bet your hair is thick, too. This style is made for thick hair."

Angel looked at her seatmate, a young girl of about thirteen. She had noticed her on the bus before, always in the same baggy jeans, gray sweatshirt and scuffed brown boots. She never would have thought she was a person who would be looking at hairstyles in a teen magazine.

"I cut hair, you know," said the girl.

"You do?"

The girl nodded. "Be glad to cut yours, if you ever want me to. I like your braid, though." She extended a hand. "I'm Audrette Taylor. I've seen you on the bus for awhile. You live in Crookwood now?"

Angel took the hand awkwardly. She had never shaken hands with a girl before. "Yes. I'm Angelsea Mead."

"I know who you are. Probably everyone does. I like your ring."

"Everyone does? Everyone who?" Angel rested her hands in her lap and nervously twisted the ring around on her finger.

"Sorry. I always exaggerate, my Gram says, and she's probably right. Everyone in Crookwood was curious about who bought the house you're living in. Of course there are only about seven people in Crookwood. Anyway, my Gram was friends with Mrs. Andrews — the woman who lived there before. She told us all about you and your family."

"We didn't buy the house. We're just renting. I don't know how long we'll be there."

"Well, I hope for my sake it's a long time. It can get lonesome out here with no one to talk to. Anyway, this is where I get off. Here — keep the magazine. In case you decide to get your hair cut that way. Nice to finally meet you." Audrette grinned and struggled off the bus with her stack of books, and Angel felt herself grinning back.

She had made a friend, just like that. And just like that, she knew what to do about Dylan's doctor.

BARBARA ELMORE

— NINE —

T H E   D E A L

As usual, Gaylon wasn't home when Angel got there. But she had left a note asking her to water the garden.

She changed her clothes, finished the chores and was sitting on the front porch at dusk when headlights brightened the driveway. It was her mother, and there was just enough light for Angel to discern her red nose and smudged mascara.

"Are you crying? What's wrong?" she demanded.

"Nothing in particular."

"Why are you crying?" Angel said, trying to hide her alarm. Her mother never cried.

"I don't want to talk about it."

"It's Dylan, isn't it? I have a right to know! Don't you ever think that not talking about anything is one of our problems?"

"What's that supposed to mean?" snapped her mother.

"What I mean is, when things get done in this family, they always seem to get done before half the family has a chance to even think about it. And we never talk about anything! It's like nothing is supposed to be a big deal, and we're supposed to keep our feelings hidden!"

"I think you have talked quite enough about your feelings. So how about you stop before I start yelling at you the way you're yelling at me?"

Their eyes locked. Struggling to calm her voice, Angel said, "I want to see Dylan. If the doctor will let me see him, I'll see the doctor."

"Turn off the water," her mother said, her voice stern, before turning on her heel and walking inside.

Angel whirled around to see the overflowing flower bed adjacent to the front porch. Right before her mother had come home, she had stuck the hose in the bed to give the plants and good soaking, and had promptly forgotten about it. She tiptoed quickly through the grass to reach the faucet and shut it off, but it did no good. Her tennis shoes were soaked through. She ripped them off at the door and stomped inside to find her mother. She wasn't going to be put off.

"I'm in the kitchen," Gaylon called. She had changed into jeans and washed her face. She looked pale and small as she cradled a mug of steaming tea, her comfort drink.

"I called the doctor. He said to tell you he doesn't like to make deals, but he will let you see Dylan. Put some shoes on. I'll take you right now.

Angel raced upstairs and stuffed her damp feet into her loafers. They felt sticky and tight, but she didn't care. Dashing for the stairs, she skidded to a halt, made a quick turn and headed for Dylan's room. It took her a moment to find his basketball, but she remembered unpacking it. Finally she found it in the back of his closet, wedged behind shoes, a model airplane and a paper bag filled with sports magazines. She scooped it up.

Her mother met her at the bottom of the stairs. "What are you going to do with that?" she asked, eyeing the basketball.

"Dylan needs it."

The two of them said nothing else until they got to the hospital forty-five minutes later.

"Angel," said her mother, touching her daughter's arm before she got out of the car. "Try not to be surprised by what you see. This place can get to you. I...I cry every day that I have to leave him here."

So that was it. Angel felt terrible for what she had said, but her mother was already out of the car, leading the way to the locked doors. In seconds they were allowed inside. Gaylon left her in the hall for a moment and went to speak to someone in an office. Then she came out and motioned to Angel. "We can't stay very long," she said as they followed a woman through more doors to a small room with two chairs, a sofa, a lamp and a table, and asked them to wait.

Angel set the basketball on the floor beside her chair, and laced her fingers together. She tapped her ring with one finger. She got up to look out the window, realized there was no window, and sat back down. She started to say something when the woman returned.

For a moment, Angel thought she had come back alone. Then Dylan appeared in the doorway. "I'll be back in ten minutes," the woman said before disappearing again.

Dylan watched the door close. He turned and sat down in a chair facing Angel and Gaylon. He didn't look at them.

"Hey, Dill. You staying out of trouble? They feed you anything good here?"

He looked at her then. "Spaghetti and meatballs for supper," he said finally.

"Was it as good as Mom's?" she said.

He shrugged.

"What do you do in here?"

"Watch TV and go to school class. Today we played baseball." He looked at the floor.

"Do you like it here?"

Angel bit her lip after asking the stupid question. But Dylan answered. "It's all right." He shrugged. "I don't care."

The woman returned and said it was time for them to go.

"But we just got here. I haven't finished talking to Dylan," Angel protested.

"We have to go, Angel," said her mother.

Angel glared at her, then looked at Dylan. He was looking at his hands. She wanted to grab him by the arm and yank him out of there.

"Well, Dill," said Angel, "I —" she stopped, remembering the basketball, which she picked up and placed in his lap. He stared at it, then at her. She bent down and gripped both arms of his chair. He didn't move.

"Listen," she whispered, her face inches from his. "You keep this, OK? It's part of your home."

His eyes stayed on her face, but he didn't smile, nod, or speak. Angel backed away, her eyes on him until she was out the door.

The visit wasn't what she had wished for, but Dylan had gained some weight back and he wasn't pale like he had been. If only he had been more like Dylan. She wouldn't say so even if tortured, but she could see why the doctor said Dylan wasn't ready to come home.

— TEN —

VISITING WITH
THE DOCTOR

Her appointment with the doctor came two days later, much to Angel's surprise. Her mother told her the night before.

"What's the rush?" Although she had made a deal, Angel still didn't want to do it.

"He's been wanting to see you for a long time, so he worked you in. Why? Do you have something else to do?"

Angel thought about making something up so she could put it off. What was she going to wear? She wanted to be mature enough to think that clothes wouldn't matter, but she feared what she wore would be a giveaway of some unpleasant character trait.

"No, Mom. I don't have anything else to do," she said, heading for her closet. After thirty minutes of rejecting skirts, blouses and pants, she finally chose a short-sleeved lemon-lime A-line dress with big blue flowers. The tags were still hanging from a sleeve as a reminder of the days she had money for clothes. "Too much, apparently," she said, looking at the dress. "Why else would I have bought this?"

She remembered when she first saw it at Amanda's Closet, a store she and Cat used to visit regularly. Instead of hanging on a rack, it was being modeled by a thin store clerk with upswept blond hair and skin resembling a porcelain doll's. On her, the dress looked elegant. Angel tried it on and decided she looked yellow and pregnant. But Cat convinced her she looked great, and the clerk had called the flowers "island blue" and told Angel they brought out her eyes. That was all she needed to hear. Angel walked out of the store with the dress, hung it in her closet and hadn't touched it since.

"Oh," said Gaylon when Angel emerged the next morning. "Is that new?"

"I've had it awhile. Just never wore it," said Angel.

"Uh-huh." Her mother didn't say anything else. They ate silently, and when Angel got up to leave, all Gaylon said was, "Remember I'll pick you up after school."

Angel chose two empty seats on the bus, hoping Audrette would sit by her. She hadn't had a chance to sit by her or say more than hello since the day Audrette gave her the magazine.

Audrette saw her as soon as she got on the bus. She waved and made her way to the empty seat. She eyed Angel's dress as she sat down. Angel saw the stare, but ignored it. She didn't know Audrette well enough to ask her what she was staring at.

"New dress?" she asked.

"Sort of. I've had it awhile. Just never wore it."

Audrette looked as if she wanted to say something else, but she didn't. To Angel's disappointment, they didn't speak the rest of the way. She couldn't say for sure, but it was almost as if the dress was a problem.

As the day wore on, Angel realized the dress was a big mistake. She spent as much time as possible hiding in the bathroom. She tried to phone her mother to ask her to bring a change of clothes, but got no answer. She was relieved when school was over.

"Hi, Honey," said Gaylon, when Angel got into the car.

"Hi," muttered Angel. "I tried to call you to ask for different clothes."

"I'm sorry. I was outside, I guess. Don't worry about the dress."

"Too late," said Angel. It was the Dress from Hell. By the time she was ushered in to see Dr. Whitfield, she was in a terrible mood. He barely glanced at the dress, but even that made her mad. She decided to focus on the bald spot at the front of his head, from which his blond hair had receded.

"Well, Angel, suppose you tell me about yourself," he said. "Do you have hobbies?"

She didn't feel like talking, but she had to be civil. No telling what he'd think about her if she was rude. But when she thought about hobbies, she realized she didn't have any. School wouldn't really count, even though it took up a lot of time. Hobbies were supposed to be the extra stuff that made you well-rounded. She'd have to make something up.

"I like to garden," she said. This wasn't one hundred percent false. She didn't dislike gardening, but she hadn't done it enough to know if she liked it, either. She wondered if he'd know she wasn't telling the truth.

"Like your mother? She likes to cook and sew, too. Do you?"

She didn't do either one of those things, either. "Oh, they're OK," she hedged. "Fashion is one of my hobbies," she said.

Dr. Whitfield decided to change the subject. "How do you feel most days, Angel? Tired, like you can't get out of bed? Or are you excited to get up and go to school?"

"Kind of in between those two. I don't jump out of bed like you see in those TV mattress commercials, but I don't drag around. I'm just an average person."

Dr. Whitfield nodded and looked at her, waiting. The silence made her nervous.

"I had a cold two weeks ago, but I didn't miss any school." Great. Now she sounded like a goody-goody.

"You like school?"

"Sometimes it's boring, but I don't know what I'd do if I didn't go. Everyone else my age has to go unless they drop out, and I don't want to do that."

"Do you have friends?"

"I used to."

"What happened?"

"We moved. It was kind of far out for them to drive." Another lie. Cat was willing to drive all over the state if it meant getting out of San Marcos. She just didn't think it was cool to be friends with someone who lived in Crookwood.

"Do you think you'll make any friends where you live now?"

"There's this one person who's nice," said Angel. "I'd like to get to know her better."

"What do you like about her?"

"She seems honest," said Angel without hesitation. "And fun."

"Uh-huh. And why do you mention honesty?"

He was on to her. He knew she wasn't a gardener. "I don't like to guess what people are thinking." He waited, but she didn't say anything else.

"Are you glad you moved to Crookwood?" the doctor asked.

"It's all right."

"That doesn't sound very enthusiastic."

"Well — the house is big, and only Mom and I live there. We need more people to fill it up, like Dylan and Dad." She chewed on the inside of her lip. Now hc would probably drag out of her all the gory details, and soon he'd know that she was the reason the family split apart.

"Did you know Dylan believes he's the cause of the family not being together?"

She had thought it for a long time, but it made her angry to hear the doctor say it. "Who made him think that?" she demanded. "Dylan had nothing to do with any of this! Who put that idea in his head?"

The doctor didn't say anything, just smiled slightly and waited.

"I just want you to tell him that," she muttered. "Tell him it was my fault, if you have to. I just want him to come home."

"Do you think it was your fault?" Dr. Whitfield asked.

She bit her lip to delay answering. If she said no, he probably wouldn't believe her. If he could tell she was lying, he might use that as a reason to keep Dylan in the hospital longer. The more she thought about what she should do, the more confused she became. Finally, she nodded wearily. "Of course it was my fault. I'm the one who lost my cool. I told my parents they should get a divorce if they couldn't stop fighting. Right after that, they sold our house and separated. I don't think they would have done it if I'd just kept my mouth shut."

"You think that happened because of what you said? Has something like that ever happened to you before? For example, have you ever said to a friend, 'I wish you'd buy me that dress?' and had her do it?"

"No," said Angel, "but it's not the same thing. That would be a joke, and what I said to my parents wasn't."

"I know you didn't mean it as a joke, Angel, but did you really want your parents to divorce? Or did you just want them to quit fighting? And do you think they had never thought about separating before that moment?"

She thought about this. She saw his point. Still, the family had come through lots of parental fights intact. Nothing changed until she butted in. "Sometimes it makes more sense to ignore things, doesn't it?" she asked. "Things that don't concern you?"

"You tell me," said the doctor. "Did you think your parents' fighting didn't concern you? When you confronted them, you obviously thought it did concern you. Think back to that time, to why you did it. Think about what you told them. I believe you spoke to them out of a very good motivation."

The doctor stared at her, perhaps waiting for more. But Angel was tired of talking about it. No matter what they said in here, her life would be the same. She might feel differently about what she did, but her parents would still be separated and Dylan would still be in the hospital.

After a few minutes of silence, the doctor checked his watch, got up and offered her his hand. "Thank you for coming, Angel. I'm glad to have met you."

She touched his hand, mumbled something and turned to leave when the ridged bottom of her shoes caught on the carpet and made her stumble forward. Dr. Whitfield reached to catch her, but she caught herself before she fell down. She felt stupid and clumsy as she plopped down between her parents in the waiting room. Before her mother could say anything, the receptionist summoned her parents, leaving Angel to sit by herself. The doctor was probably telling them that she needed help more than Dylan did. Her stupid-looking dress proved that, if nothing else had.

When her parents finally emerged, their solemn faces worried her. She got in her mother's car while her parents stood and talked, their faces serious. Angel rolled down the window, desperately trying to hear them, but she couldn't make out the words because of traffic noise. Then her parents hugged and her father came to the car and kissed Angel on the top of the head. She and her mother drove home silently, Angel burning with questions she was afraid to ask.

At school the next day, she noticed people whispering when she walked by. Or they'd stop talking when she drew near. The first two times she thought she was imagining it, but after it happened the third time, she knew something was up.

She saw Audrette at lunch on the lawn outside. She was alone, so Angel asked if she could eat with her.

"Sure," said Audrette. "Who wants to eat alone?"

For awhile they ate silently. When Audrette crunched a carrot stick, Angel came out of her reverie. "People are whispering about me," she said.

"That's weird," said Audrette. "Maybe it's your imagination." Her words belied the guilty look on her face.

"No, it's not. It's happened too many times to be my imagination. And you know something," Angel said.

"What do you mean?"

"I can tell from your face. You know why they're whispering. What have you heard?"

"Nothing."

"If you want to be my friend, tell me."

"It'll blow over, Angelsea. Next week it will be something else. Believe me. I've been through this."

"If you don't tell me right now, I'll leave and never speak to you again!"

"All right," said Audrette, reluctantly. She took a deep breath. "There's a rumor going around that you're pregnant."

"Pregnant!" Angel yelled. Another group of girls a few feet away turned to stare. They got up in unison and moved away, as if they feared catching something.

"Yelling isn't going to help," said Audrette.

Angel staring at the air in front of her. She felt like someone had drained her blood. "Everyone thinks I'm pregnant?" she said, mostly to herself. "How could they?" Then her eyes widened as she realized exactly how. "The dress?" she asked Audrette.

Audrette wouldn't look at her, but she nodded.

"Oh my God!" said Angel. "That's all it took?"

"No, that's not all it took," Audrette said, an angry edge to her voice. "No one would have thought it was anything more than an ugly dress, except someone got the rumor started."

"Who?" demanded Angel. "Who would do such a thing?" Audrette just stared at her, waiting for her to figure it out. "Oh no," groaned Angel when the realization hit her. She wrapped her arms around her knees and lowered her head to hide her face.

Audrette didn't say anything. After awhile, Angel raised her head and looked at her. She wasn't eating, either, just staring off into the distance. "Why do you think she'd do it?" Angel asked, her voice almost a whisper.

"She probably didn't need a reason."

After school, they sat together on the bus, silent. Angel spoke when the bus was almost to Audrette's stop. "So what do I do now?"

"There's not much you can do. It'll be obvious soon that you're not pregnant."

"Yeah, but how does that prove I never was?"

"You can't prove it," said Audrette. "The people who know you won't buy it anyway. The ones who don't know you — who cares about them?"

"You'd care if it were you," muttered Angel.

There was a long pause, then Audrette responded, "You're right. Remember when I said I had dealt with this before? I was at a private school before this one. Gram thought it would be better for me. We couldn't afford it, but my grades got me in on scholarship. Anyway, kids there made up a lie about me. I didn't have any friends, and I thought that everyone believed it. I could break up a crowd in ten seconds. There were days when I felt like killing myself."

"What was the lie?"

"They said I was a lesbian. I think it was because of my clothes — I don't dress up much. They said Gram was one, too. That it ran in the family. I think that made me madder than the lies they told about me. I mean, why would anyone bring Gram into it?"

Angel shook her head. "What did your Mom say?"

"I don't have a mother. It's just Gram and me. My father left my mom when I was a baby, and then my mom got killed in a wreck. So Gram raised me since I was a toddler."

Angel didn't know what to say. Audrette obviously didn't ache for parents she had never known, but it couldn't be easy to be raised by her grandmother. Her own problems suddenly seemed very small. "I don't understand why people do things like that," she said weakly.

Audrette shrugged. "I think it makes them feel powerful to have everyone listen to them. They get a lot of attention. And the people they're making up the stories about don't matter to them because they don't ever have to face the harm they do."

She was wise beyond her years. Angel had run with the "right" people and had never before been the victim of rumors. But she had heard rumors about other kids, had even believed them. She probably had passed some on. Gossiping was a big pastime at San Marcos High.

She learned a lot about the power of gossip over the next couple of weeks, about its viciousness and the ease with which it oozed everywhere and clung, like a poisonous syrup. In computer class, someone sent her an anonymous email: "A.M. — Any morning sickness?" When she began looking around the room for the guilty party, almost everyone began to snicker. The email had gone out to the whole class.

Right before lunch period one day, a folded piece of paper fell out of her locker. Someone had jammed it in the bottom. She was afraid to open it and afraid not to. Without showing her fear, she unfolded it right there in the crowded hall. It was an ode to Angelsea Mead, with ode spelled "oad." The poem, in Cat's handwriting, was filled with crude rhymes and misspelled words.

After reading it, Angel looked up. Dozens of eyes stared back at her expectantly, and giggles erupted here and there. She saw three guys, one of them Cat's current boyfriend, high-fiving each other. Cat was nowhere around, of course.

Adrenalin surging, she headed toward the three boys. The giggling stopped, and people in the hall parted quickly, making a path. The trio stayed put, but they exchanged nervous glances. Obviously they had not expected her to confront them.

Angel held the note out to them with the tips of two fingers, as if it were soiled. "You all were so obviously pleased for me to get this that I can't help but think one of you knows the author. I'm going to let you give it back to that person. Please tell her that the written word has more effect when the writer knows how to spell." She smiled sweetly and tucked the note into the pocket of Chad Mercer, Cat's boyfriend.

She turned and made her way back through the crowd of open-mouthed students. She hurried to the restroom, where she promptly threw up.

— ELEVEN —

A RUMOR
COMES AND GOES

Audrette was right about the pregnancy rumor. It died away almost as quickly as it had been given life. Angel was glad that her mother never heard about it. In town, the moms' network had been strong and Gaylon would've heard about the rumor the day it started. She had lost her network in the move to Crookwood, and was never home for anyone to call her anyway because of Dylan's illness.

One good result of the rumor was that Angel and Audrette had become friends, one always saving a seat for the other on the bus. Their friendship hadn't yet grown beyond the school bus stage, but their time spent on the bus allowed them to compare notes about homework, teachers, and occasionally about hair and clothes.

"Angel," Audrette asked her one day as they rode home, "have you ever had a boyfriend?"

"No — I've gone out a couple of times. But not since we moved. We live too far out."

"Even if someone really liked you?"

"I don't know anyone who likes me that much."

"Is there anyone you like?"

"There's someone I think I could like," said Angel, blushing. "But I don't think he even knows I'm alive."

"Who is it?"

"He's a senior. He takes pictures for the yearbook. And he runs track."

"Who is it?" persisted Audrette. "Tell me!"

"You promise you won't tell anyone?"

"Who would I tell, Angel? You're my only friend!"

"Clifton Neal. Do you know him?"

For a brief moment, Angel thought she saw surprise flicker across Audrette's face. Then she decided she must have imagined it.

"Yes, I know who he is. He's cute, if you like handsome blonds."

"He is cute, but it's more than just that. He's always nice to everyone, even when he doesn't know them. He seems very kind."

Audrette nodded thoughtfully.

"What about you? Do you like anyone?"

Audrette didn't answer. She was staring into space, a million miles away. "Audrette? What are you thinking about?"

"About boys. Trying to think of any I know who are worthy of me. There aren't any."

"Then maybe you'd consider going to the spring dance with me. I've gone since I was thirteen, and I don't want to miss it this year. It's fun even if you don't have a date."

"I don't think so, Angel."

"Why not?"

"I just don't fit in at stuff like that. Look at me. I can't believe you'd want me to go with you to any dress-up social function."

"Of course I would," said Angel without hesitation. "Don't let clothes stop you from going — we'd find you something to wear. You'd look really good in green, by the way."

"If I agreed to go – and I'm not saying I would – would you let me cut your hair?"

"Let me think about it. I'm not a person to get my hair cut on impulse."

Audrette nodded. "OK. And when you come out to the house," she said as if Angel had already agreed, "you can meet Gram. She's anxious to meet you because I talk about you all the time."

Angel thought about having Audrette cut her hair for almost a week. She finally decided her single braid was outdated and that Audrette couldn't make matters much worse. She told Audrette that day, and they scheduled the hair-cutting for Audrette's house the next day after school.

Angel's stomach was full of butterflies by the time she got off the bus with Audrette. She felt like a volcano about to erupt. To make matters worse, Audrette stole glances at her hair every time they were together.

She had never seen Audrette's house from the bus. It was set far from the road behind a stand of oak and cedar trees, and their arrival was announced by a sudden, ferocious barking. Angel searched for the source of the noise and saw the house gleaming white in the late-afternoon sun. It appeared to be smaller and newer than her family's. The trimmed grass was sprouting green. Bearded irises preened in front of a white picket fence, and a large silvery bush graced one corner of the yard.

Then she spied a huge black dog. It bounded off the front porch, ears flying. He charged at Angel and Audrette. The dog skidded to a halt at Audrette's side, and she leaned down to scratch his ears. Angel cautiously held out her hand for him to sniff. He licked it, and she laughed out loud.

"Doncha harm that dog," drawled a voice.

Angel looked up to see an old woman staring at her, leaning on a shotgun. Her face and hands were tan and as wrinkled as soft cotton. She wore a long-sleeved chambray shirt, denim overalls and heavy boots. A few strands of wispy gray hair straggled from beneath a huge straw hat, tied onto her head with a floppy red bow which looked out of place.

"Gram," said Audrette, "I've told you a dozen times you shouldn't bring that shotgun to the road. At least not when I bring a friend home. This is Angelsea Mead. Angel, this is my grandmother, Romie Taylor. You'll have to excuse her — she doesn't like strangers."

"You talk too much!" the old woman snapped. "And you!" she said to Angel, "you'd better come inside and have something to eat. You're too skinny for as tall as you are, and you'll need your strength to walk home. Don't expect me to drive you." She turned and headed up the sidewalk.

"You're safer walking anyway," Audrette said in a low voice.

"Audie, I heard that!" said her grandmother.

Audrette grinned at Angel, who was laughing. As soon as she stepped into the house, she felt at home. From the doorway her eye was drawn to a ceiling fan circling lazily overhead, drawing her attention to the beamed ceiling. The walls and floor were all the same honey-brown color, and a braided rug of mostly blue covered the floor. White curtains with blue trim hung over the windows. Following Audrette and trying to see everything, she almost missed the dolls lined up on the fireplace mantel. She gaped at them. There must be dozens.

Seeing her stare, Audrette went to the mantel, picked up one of the dolls and handed it to Angel. The figure was a woman with a tiny hoe. The image of Romie, she was dressed in a long checked dress. Her hair, made of brown yarn, was braided and wound into a bun on the back of her head. Her body and head were made of material Angel didn't recognize. Her delicate face — black eyebrows, hazel eyes and red lips — had been painted on.

"What's she made of?" Angel asked.

"Corn husks. Gram's dolls are a surprise to everyone."

"How many of them are there?" Angel asked, staring at the dozens of different faces.

"We lost count. There are more in the closets. She makes them in the winter when it gets dark so early that you can't do anything outside. She doesn't watch television."

"And I don't sell 'em!" yelled Romie, who was holding open the swinging door to the kitchen. "I only give 'em away to deserving people. C'mon, you two!" she said, snatching off her hat.

Angel gently placed the doll back on the mantel and followed Audrette into the huge kitchen. Romie patted her hand. "I'm sorry I came at you with a shotgun, child, but the last stranger who came up my front walk was a magazine salesman who kicked Boone."

"Boone's the dog," Audrette said. "He dropped by one day about ten years ago and never left."

"Think you'll keep him?" Angel asked Romie.

"Hee-hee! I can see why you like her, Audie! She has a sense of humor. Sit down, Angelsea. You hungry? We'll have tea and cookies. I understand you're getting a haircut today?"

Angel nodded. "You've got the best hairstylist in Crookwood," said Romie. " 'Course she's the only one, too," she said with a chuckle. "Where'd you get a name like Angelsea?"

Angel saw immediately where Audrette's directness came from. "My Mom and Dad named me after a song they liked."

"Your parents buy Mrs. Andrews' place?" Romie asked.

"We're leasing it, but my mom wants to buy it."

"Just your mom? What about your dad?"

"Gram!" scolded Audrette.

Angel smiled. "It's all right, Audrette. He isn't living with us — my parents are separated. And my brother is in the hospital. So right now, it's just Mom and me." The words came out easier than she'd imagined.

"I'm sorry, child," murmured Romie, looking into her teacup. Everyone was silent a moment before she blurted, "What's the matter with your brother?"

"Gram!" yelled Audrette, rolling her eyes.

"Hush, you! This is how you learn things. Better than listening to gossip!"

Angel liked her thinking. "He got sick because of the family splitting up. He was afraid he wasn't going to have a family anymore. And somehow he got everything twisted up and thinks it's all his fault."

Romie nodded slowly. "Kids are like that," she said. "When he gets out of the hospital, you bring him over here. We'll all have tea and cookies!"

After they had finished their snack, Romie chased them out of the kitchen, saying she had work to do. "Don't worry," she said to Angel, "you're in good hands. Audie knows what she's doing."

The reassurance wasn't enough to keep Angel from being nervous as she sat in a high-backed dining table chair in Audrette's tiny bedroom. She stared at herself in an old mirror. She was as pale as the white sheet shrouding her shoulders. She had unbraided her hair and washed it in the bathroom sink. "Let's do this," she said to Audrette, who was moving from side to side, lifting up strands of Angel's hair.

"I've got to get an idea of the finished look, Angel, or else I'll botch it."

Angel closed her eyes. "Please don't say words like botch."

Romie's chuckle drifted in from the kitchen.

"Gram!" yelled Audrette in a threatening tone. "Stop it!" When the chuckling continued, Audrette slammed the bedroom door. "You're going to have to trust me Angel. Have a little faith."

"How many people have been led to slaughter with those words?"

"Oh, quit being so dramatic," Audrette said. "And no mirrors," she added. "You have to turn the chair to face the other way. If you watch while I'm cutting, I'll get nervous and mess up."

"But I'll get nervous if I don't look. What if I don't like what you're doing and want to stop you before it's too late?"

Audrette shrugged. "Hair grows back."

Angel tugged at the sheet, trying to get it off. "That's it!" she cried. "Never mind!"

Audrette put up her hands. "I'm sorry. I'm just trying to get you not to be so nervous. It'll be all right. I promise. Cross my heart and hope to die."

Angel eyed Audrette like she was a mad dog, then sighed and turned her chair away from the mirror. She sat down, closed her eyes and nodded. "All right. Hurry before I change my mind." Next she heard snipping and felt pieces of hair drifting to her shoulders, into her lap. She tried to relax, but she was clenching her teeth so hard her head began to hurt. As the clicking sound of scissors continued and she felt more and more locks of hair drifting down, she began to despair of having anything left on her head.

After thirty minutes, just when she had decided she couldn't take the clink and jingle of scissors any longer, Audrette switched on a blow-dryer and began flicking her hands through Angel's hair. After a few minutes, the dryer stopped and she announced, "All done!"

Angel's eyes flew open. "You're finished?"

Audrette nodded as she reached out to arrange a lock. "I went slow. I wanted to make sure I did it right. You look different."

"Good different?" Angel started to turn to look in the mirror, but Audrette stopped her with an upraised hand. She backed to the door and opened it. "Gram!" she yelled. "Come see!"

Romie stepped in a moment later, wiping her hands on her apron, and stared at Angel, face expressionless. Silently she circled the chair, then put a finger under Angel's chin and turned her head one way, then the other. She looked at Audrette, nodded once, then winked at Angel and walked out.

"What did that mean?" asked Angel.

Audrette handed her a big round mirror. "See for yourself."

Angel looked, and gasped.

"Well?" Audrette asked nervously.

Angel got up and turned around to stare in the big mirror, to get the full effect. Her hair had never been this short. Audrette had feathered it on top, cut it short over the ears and tapered it in the back.

"It isn't the cut I showed you in the magazine. I changed my mind. You have a cowlick here, so I cut the hair around the front of your head to play off that. You also have fine hair that feathers easily, so this cut is perfect for it. In the back, it wanted to kick out. So I tapered it. What do you think?"

Angel couldn't explain how she felt. She looked both older and younger at the same time.

"Angel? Do you absolutely hate it?"

"Oh, no," Angel breathed, tearing her eyes away from the mirror to look at Audrette. "It's the best haircut I've ever had."

"It is? No kidding?"

Angel nodded, staring into the mirror again. "How did you learn to do this?"

"Reading. Looking at pictures. And I used to practice on Gram, before she decided she didn't want her hair cut any more. I imagined for a long time what I'd do to yours."

"You know you'll have to keep cutting it now. You can't have a hairstyle like this just one time and let it go. And I can't afford to go to a stylist."

Audrette shrugged and whipped the sheet off Angel, careful not to get any hair on her. "Guess this means we're friends for life then," she said. Abruptly, Angel hugged her then backed away. They stood in embarrassed silence.

"Got a broom? I'll sweep up the hair," Angel offered. Audrette disappeared and returned with a broom and dustpan. Their embarrassment slowly faded.

After dancing around Romie in the kitchen, Angel told Audrette goodbye and headed home with a jar of Romie's canned tomatoes. When she got home, she found her mother in a cleaning frenzy.

"Hello," Gaylon called over the whine of the vacuum cleaner as she heard the front door close. "I wanted everything shipshape. Dylan's coming home tomorrow!"

"He is?" yelled Angel. "Does that mean he's OK?"

Her mother was in the front room with her back to the door, hurriedly pushing the vacuum back and forth. "Guess so. The doctor said we should pick him up about two." She turned around to glance at her daughter, looked away and back again, then turned off the vacuum and walked over to Angel. She made a circle around her as Romie had done, looking at the hair from every angle.

"I thought you were going to Audrette's house after school."

"I did. You like my hair?"

"It's wonderful," said Gaylon, "and it suits you. So I hate ask, but how did you pay for it? A cut like this is expensive."

"It was free, Mom. Audrette did it."

Her mother didn't believe her at first, but Angel finally convinced her, then told her about the deal they had made.

"That's a good idea," her mother said. "I guess it's time I met Audrette. From what you've told me about her, I didn't think she was your type. But maybe I was wrong."

"What is my type?"

"Oh, someone like Catherine, popular, pretty —"

"Spoiled and selfish?"

Her mother smiled. "I didn't say that. Anyway, Audrette definitely sounds different from Cat. She sounds like she has a mind of her own. I'd like to meet her."

"OK. Can I go with you to get Dylan?"

"I think that can be arranged. Meanwhile, I need you to help me clean the house. I want it spic and span for tomorrow."

Dylan wouldn't know dirt if it tapped him on the shoulder, but Angel cheerfully helped her mother clean. She would have built Dylan his own house just to get him back home.

— TWELVE —

DYLAN'S HOME!

Dylan was home a little over a week when Angel decided either he needed to go back to the hospital or she would go herself just to get away from him. He was driving her crazy, and for that matter, so was Gaylon.

When Dylan was awake and at home, he demanded constant attention. He wanted to be where Angel was all the time, but only to call her names — Giraffe seemed to be his favorite — or tell lies about her to Gaylon. Or he "borrowed" her things without asking. Like the Walkman she had gotten for Christmas, which mysteriously disappeared from the top right dresser drawer where she kept it.

"Dylan, did you take my Walkman?" she asked him one Saturday morning, only the second weekend he'd been home. He was watching cartoons on television and didn't answer or even turn around.

"Dylan," Angel said, her voice louder, "I can't find my Walkman. Did you take it?" She nudged his foot with hers.

Suddenly, Dylan rolled around on the floor, screaming in pain. Gaylon came running in. "What's going on?" she demanded, looking at Angel, who was watching Dylan in stunned silence.

"Beats me."

"She kicked me!" Dylan wailed. "All I did was borrow her Walkman, and she kicked me!"

Gaylon looked at her in horror before kneeling down to check the knee Dylan was holding in apparent agony. Dylan glanced at Angel over her head.

"I don't see anything Dylan. Where does it hurt?" asked Gaylon.

"Yeah, Dill, where does it hurt?" asked Angel, her voice dripping sarcasm. This wasn't the first time since he'd come home that Dylan had pulled such a stunt. He'd faked illness more than once after dinner, always on his night to do the dishes. When it was his turn to mow the lawn, he told Gaylon that the mower's fumes made him sick and that he was scared of cutting off his toes. When he started crying, she told Angel to mow the lawn.

He didn't even make up his own bed. After twice putting the spread on sideways and once wrong side up, Gaylon either did it herself or asked Angel to.

"Angel, I cannot believe you kicked your little brother," said Gaylon, getting up. "I've never known you to hurt him before."

Angel stared at her. Apparently her mother was losing her mind, too. "Hold that thought, Mom. It'll be something good for you to remember when I start kicking him regularly, which, by the way, I haven't done yet. What do you say, Dylan? How about a good swift kick in the butt? I've heard it's a cure for lying."

Dylan jumped up and ran out of the room screaming, while Gaylon stared at Angel as if she were a stranger. "How can you treat your little brother with so little compassion, Angelsea Mead? He has gone through a rough time of it, and I expect more from you. You are the oldest — and I thought you were the most mature."

"Sorry, Mom. I didn't know that meant I was supposed to let him lie about me without mentioning it. So are we supposed to ignore every bit of his bad behavior? Because that could be a full-time job. I might even have to drop out of school to keep up with the chores that Dylan is too sick to do."

For a moment, Angel sensed her mother was going to slap her. But Gaylon instead clinched her fists and stalked out of the room.

Dylan and Audrette didn't get along, either. The first time Dylan met her was on the school bus, where he was sitting next to Angel. "Dill, this is my friend

Audrette, and we want to sit together," she told him. "There's a vacant seat across the aisle."

"I like this seat," he said, refusing to even look at Audrette.

"That one's just the same, and the boy sitting there looks nice. You ought to get to know him. Besides, I see you all the time. I hardly ever see Audrette. So move!"

He did, but she didn't like the glint she saw in his eyes. That night, he told Gaylon that Angel wouldn't sit next to him on the bus because she was embarrassed to have a brother who had been "in the nuthouse."

After a loud, lengthy lecture from Gaylon, Angel stopped by his room. He was pretending to read, but she knew he had strained to hear every word. "You were right that time, Dylan. I am completely embarrassed by you. But I'm more embarrassed for you, that you think you have to do these things to get attention."

No matter how poorly she was getting along with Dylan, Angel was looking forward to a family dinner that Gaylon had planned to celebrate Dylan's homecoming. It included only them and Gary, but an air of festivity filled the house the Friday afternoon before he got there. Angel found herself hoping he would spend the weekend. It would be the first time they had all been together in months. And maybe he could straighten out Dylan.

Before dinner, she combed her hair half a dozen times. She wanted to look perfect. She applied mascara carefully, put on a white T-shirt and the blue shorts her mother had recently made her and went downstairs to see if her mother needed help.

"You look lovely, Angel," her mother said.

"Thanks." Angel blushed. She hadn't been expecting a compliment — there had been few lately — and the word "lovely" hadn't come to mind, although she'd thought she looked pretty good. She usually was too skinny and clumsy, her hair too mousy brown and the angles on her face too prominent. But for a short while she felt statuesque instead of gangly and had good cheekbones instead of an angular face. "Maybe I should go try on that yellow A-line again."

"I threw it out," said her mother, smiling.

"I thought I heard Dad drive up. Where is he?"

"Out putting up a basketball hoop on the garage. It's a present for Dylan."

Angel heard a familiar thump and looked upstairs. Dylan was coming down with his basketball, bouncing it on each step. Bouncing a basketball in the house was something Gaylon would never have allowed before.

He ran outside before anyone could say anything, and he and Gary shot baskets for at least twenty minutes before Gaylon summoned them to eat her lasagna, Dylan's favorite.

"Gaylon," said Gary between bites, "I haven't seen the house since before you moved. It looks really nice. What have you done out here?" Angel looked at him warily before deciding he wasn't trying to start a fight. She glanced at her mother. She held her breath.

"Well, let's see," Gaylon said. "You know about the new roof because you helped pay for it. We've cleaned up the yard and planted a garden. The grass — what there is of it — our daughter has been mowing. We painted the outside. We still have a lot to do, but it's coming along."

For a moment, the only sound was chewing and Angel wondered if everyone else was thinking the same thing she was, that it wasn't such a bad place. Then Dylan blurted, "So, Dad, are you going to move out here or not? Because it doesn't sound to me like Mom's going anywhere. Or are you going to get a divorce?"

His impudence was so breathtaking Angel didn't know whether to laugh or gasp. She stuffed food in her mouth and observed everyone else. Her father gulped down a forkful of lasagna without chewing, and started coughing as it caught in his throat. Gaylon accidentally banged her tea glass on the edge of the table, almost breaking it.

"Dylan," Gaylon said, "how could you know what I'm going to do when I don't even know? And who ever said anything about divorce?"

"It's true, isn't it? You aren't moving back to town, are you?" he asked.

"I think that depends a lot on the rest of the family," she said.

"What if I don't want to live here?" Dylan demanded. "What if I wanted to live with Dad?"

Angel pushed her plate away. She had lost her appetite.

"If that's the way you feel..." Gaylon didn't finish. She sounded calm, but she was twisting her napkin into a ball. "Is that what you want to do, Dylan?"

He looked down at his plate, which was half-full, and shrugged.

Nobody talked much after that. Angel had hoped dinner would end so late that her father would stay over. Instead, she ended up clearing the table while everyone else — including Dylan — disappeared. She was putting away the last plate when she heard a car start. A moment later her mother came in from the porch.

Gaylon hugged Angel from behind, her cheek on the top of her daughter's head. Angel was almost too tall for her mother to do that any more.

"I figured if I waited long enough, you'd have it all cleaned up."

Angel pulled away. "Dad left?"

"Yes. Said he had to work tomorrow, on a Saturday. That's your dad."

"What if Dylan really does want to live with him?" Angel blurted.

Her mother's face didn't change, and she sounded calm. "I don't know. It's something we need to discuss."

"Would you let him do it or not?" Angel pressed. But her mother was silent so long that Angel decided she wasn't going to answer. She was turning to go to her room when Gaylon finally spoke.

"I want my children to live with me," she said.

It wasn't a yes or no, but it would have to do. Angel said she was tired and headed for her bedroom, taking the steps two at a time. She glanced at Dylan's door. It was closed, but a strip of light shone underneath. She wondered for a moment if she should disturb him, then decided she was being silly.

In a fit of politeness, she knocked on his door. When there was no answer, she rapped harder. Still no answer. She had her hand on the knob and was getting ready to push open the door when he asked, "Who is it?"

"Countess Dracula," Angel said.

"Enter," he said. His voice told her his mood had lowered a notch. He was sitting on his bed, facing the window. His legs were stretched out in front of him, crossed at the ankles. Angel was surprised at how tall he was getting. One day he'd be taller than she was. She didn't like that. She was used to being the biggest as well as the oldest.

"I had to clean up the kitchen all by myself. You owe me. You owe me for a lot, in fact." She sat down beside him.

"I should get freebies. I've been sick."

"You got freebies the whole time you were gone," she said, trying to keep her voice light. She meant was she was saying, but she wanted Dylan to hear her, not shut her out. "If I were to add them up and make you pay me back, you'd be through about the time you graduated from college. But I won't do that because I'm nice. I just want you to be grateful — and owe me — for the rest of your life."

"Full moon tonight," said Dylan, leaving her to wonder whether anything had registered. "You know what they say about crazy people and a full moon?" He stretched his upper lip over his teeth as if to bare a set of fangs and turned toward her.

"That you're as ugly by the light of a full moon as you are in broad daylight?"

He shook his head in mock disgust. "Angel, do you think there's something wrong with me?"

"Yep. I think you have to be at least half-goofy to be a part of this family. Besides, your real parents were from another planet. Mom and Dad rescued you when you were three. So I guess we could say you were adopted. But don't tell anyone."

Dylan ignored her joke. "I used to think I made Mom and Dad split up," he said.

"Yeah, I know."

"Then I got real afraid that I'd lose Mom and Dad both."

"That's all silly! You didn't do anything! It was me! Don't you get it?" She stopped abruptly, and Dylan looked at her.

"You? What did you do?"

"Nothing. Never mind. This is a dumb conversation. You didn't cause what happened to them."

He sighed. "I still wish they'd get back together."

"I do, too." Angel stood up and lightly rubbed her knuckles on his scalp. Dylan didn't look up and didn't say good night.

That night, she dreamed she was tried at a school assembly for making her parents break up and for beating up Dylan. The whole school voted, and she was found guilty. Harmon Bradford was the judge. Just as she was about to announce the sentence, Angel woke up sweating and couldn't go back to sleep.

—— THIRTEEN ——

O N C E   A   M O N S T E R ...

Angel thought Dylan would snap out of his monster period, but it didn't happen. She had to content herself with the times he was fine. The rest of the time he went into a sort of trance, where he didn't see or hear much that went on around him. When he got like that, you had to yell at him to get his attention. And then he was hateful.

Audrette refused to put up with what she called his "spells". She said Dylan was spoiled and selfish, and that he was encouraged to be that way because Gaylon gave him whatever he wanted. And she got angry when Angel couldn't come over to her house without bringing Dylan. That was Gaylon's rule when she wasn't home.

"You can't bring Dylan here," Audrette said one Saturday afternoon after calling Angel to ask her over. "Gram would shoot him if he acted hateful around her. On second thought, maybe you should bring him."

"Why don't you come over here instead?" asked Angel.

"I don't want to be around your brother."

"I don't blame you, but he's in his room playing on his computer right now. He won't bother us. We could look at dresses in magazines and get ideas for the spring dance."

Audrette agreed, and in a few minutes she was there. She was out of breath, having run the whole two miles between their houses. Angel fixed them Cokes and put some brownies on a plate, and they sat in the kitchen looking at Seventeen, Glamour and other magazines.

"The dance is just weeks away," Angel said. "We need to decide what we're going to wear."

"It all looks like a lot of trouble," said Audrette, eyeing a one-shouldered fuschia dress in one of the magazines. "You have to have the right shoes, and a bag, and you have to get your hair done. I never said I was going."

"Yes you did. It was part of our deal," bantered Angel good-naturedly.

Dylan came into the kitchen and reached for the last brownie. Angel grabbed his hand. "That's Audrette's. It's the last one. You ate most of them."

"So? Mom made them for me," said Dylan.

"I don't think so."

"Why does she need the last one?" asked Dylan.

"For my strength," said Audrette. She took the brownie and put it whole into her mouth. Angel started giggling. Dylan's eyes got dark with anger, as he watched Audrette chew and swallow.

"Delicious," she said, licking her fingers.

"You know what, Audrette?" said Dylan. "You probably shouldn't go to the dance. Who would dance with you anyway? You ought to hear what they call you at school — Beverly Hillbilly!" Then he made a face at her and ran out of the room.

Angel glanced at her friend's red face and shook her head. "I'm sorry, Audrette. He's an absolute brat."

"That's it?" Audrette exploded. "That's all you have to say? A wimpy "I'm sorry" and nothing to Dylan about being hateful?"

"It wouldn't do any good, believe me. Hey, where are you going?"

"Home," said Audrette.

"But why? You just got here."

"If you don't know, I'm not going to tell you." She left with a slam of the front door.

Angel stared after her for a long time. She did know, and she couldn't blame Audrette. She should have stuck up for her. It was just easier sometimes to ignore Dylan and apologize for him.

At school Monday, Audrette avoided her all day, even at lunch. As she ate her sandwich alone, Angel tried to focus on a book she'd brought with her. She quit after reading the same sentence over and over.

When she got on the bus after school, Audrette was already there, staring out the window. She was alone, so Angel sat down beside her.

"Hi," Angel said.

"Hi yourself." Audrette turned around to look at Angel.

"You look down. What's the matter?" Angel asked.

"What do you mean, what's the matter? The matter is that I'm disappointed. I thought you were my friend."

Dylan got on the bus and glared at Audrette, who glared back. Neither of them said anything. He took a seat in the back.

"I am your friend. I'm sorry for what Dylan said to you." Angel said. "He had no right."

Audrette sniffed. "Big deal. Same old Dylan. I don't expect much from him. But I do from you."

"I have some expectations, too," said Angel, growing angry. "I expect you to know that Dylan's gone through a rough time, and that we are both doing the best we can. He's not always like this."

Audrette shrugged. "Whatever you say. Seems to me you're blind to who he really is. I think he's spoiled rotten."

Angel clenched her teeth. "I don't think you know —"

"Why can't you admit it, Angel? He's always like this. He forgets his books, and you have to go get them. He doesn't pay attention to anyone talking to him.

Your mom is always taking him somewhere to do something only he likes to do, like miniature golf. He gets away with murder, and no one ever says anything to him. I thought after awhile it would end, that no one would put up with it. But no one in your family ever seems to move forward. It's like you're all stuck in place. I guess it runs in the family."

"I am sorry we don't measure up to your high Crookwood standards," snapped Angel. "I had no idea everyone you know is so perfect. Since I disappoint you so much, maybe we should just forget about being friends."

Audrette looked at her once before turning away. Angel got up and found another seat. Just before Audrette got off at her stop, she looked back at Angel once, as if to say goodbye. Then she was gone.

Angel wanted to call after her, say she was sorry, that she didn't really mean it. But it was too late. Audrette was walking as fast as she could with her load of books, her shoulders slumped. The sight of her stumbling down the rutted road made Angel feel awful.

She and Dylan got off a few minutes later at their own house. Angel stood beside the road staring at the bus as it rumbled down the road. She wasn't really seeing it; she was still seeing Audrette, with her shoulders rounded forward, her head down, hurrying home. She had hurt the best friend she'd ever had. How'd they get to this point so suddenly?

She was brought back to the present by Dylan tugging on her arm.

"What do you want?" Angel snapped, swinging around to face him.

"Let's go. I want to go home."

"We are home. It's right there. If you pull on my arm like that again, I'm going to punch you out. Got it?" She expected him to pout, but she didn't care. He was to blame for her fight with Audrette.

They started walking toward the house, and Angel glanced at Dylan. He looked back at her, then made a face, the kind Angel hated, tugging down at the skin under his eyes and pushing up on his nose until he resembled a pig with the flu.

"Stop it! You know I hate that!"

"What'll you do if I don't?"

She didn't say anything, and he made the face again. She reached out to grab one of his arms, but he started running. Angel threw down her books and chased him. Running on adrenaline, she caught him easily. But keeping his flailing arms from hitting her was another matter. Finally, she wrapped them with her own. When she had him stomach-down on the ground, her knees on his rump, she ordered him to give up.

"OK, OK! I give!"

Angel got off his back and sat in the grass. Dylan rolled upright and sat beside her, arms hugging his knees. For a moment, they were quiet. She sensed he was waiting for her to say something, so she did.

"You've got to start acting like a human being, Dylan. Life isn't just about what you want. Audrette is — was — my best friend, and because I didn't stick up for her when you were mean, we had a big fight. Now I don't know if she'll ever speak to me again. It would serve me right if she didn't." She expected him to pout. He surprised her.

"I know. I'm sorry," he said. "It's just that some-times I feel so sad, and then I start feeling like I'm a creep, and then I can't help what I do."

"Does the doctor know you feel like this?" she asked.

"I don't know. No, I guess not."

"You should tell him next time you see him."

"What if it means I have to go back to the hospital? I don't want to go back there."

"You don't feel sad all the time, do you?"

Dylan shook his head.

"Well then, he probably won't put you in the hospi-tal. But even if he did, maybe it would be better than the sadness. Maybe he could help you get rid of it. He helped you before." She could tell he was considering this. After a moment he sighed, from somewhere deep within.

"I don't ever want to go back there," he said again. "They weren't terrible to me or anything. I felt like...I didn't belong there. Or anywhere. You know?"

She nodded even though she could only guess.

"I think I caused Mom and Dad to fight," he said. "I always wanted Dad to do something with me when he was home, and I always wanted Mom to cook special things for dinner. I'm probably the one who caused them to split up."

She shook her head. Dylan, that's just wrong. You didn't cause them to fight, or to break up, and I can prove it."

"How?"

"They used to fight way before you were born."

"About what?"

"Let's see...one time, Mom was painting the eaves of the house and forgot she was supposed to go with Dad to a party and she had paint in her hair and couldn't get it out. That fight was a killer. He accused of her getting paint in her hair on purpose." She shook her head, remembering. "There was her Save the Tree protest. That happened the same time he was planning on running for city council, and he thought nobody would vote for him because his wife was a nut. They yelled so loud at each other, I thought the police would come. She threatened to leave him that time, but she didn't."

"Are you making this up?"

"How could I make it up? It's too weird. Listen, Dylan, there's no way you could have caused the fighting or the breakup. Their fights started long before you ever got here. And there's no way you could have prevented them, either. I tried that myself."

"So you think when they told us that they were separating because they didn't want the same things, they meant it?"

"Yes," she said, surprising herself. "Yes, I think that's exactly what they meant."

"Angel," he said after a moment, "have you ever thought about running away?"

She looked at him, considering. "Sure. Everyone does, I think. But thinking about it is different from actually doing it."

"I daydream about it sometimes, when I can't think of anything else to do. I think maybe it would bring Mom and Dad back together. You know — like they'd team up to find me?"

"Uh-huh. And as soon as they found you, they'd be apart again. See, if we didn't make them come apart, we can't put them back together," said Angel.

"But what are we going to do?"

"Manage," she said, brushing dust off her sneaker.

He nodded. "I'm really sorry about Audrette."

"Me, too. If you ever pull anything with her again, I'll deck you. I mean it." She bit her lip as she realized she probably wouldn't get another chance to defend Audrette. But there was no use brooding over it. "Hey, want to make it up to me?"

"How?"

"Wash Mom's car. She wanted me to do it after school. I'm sure it's your turn."

He frowned. "But I've been sick."

"You don't look sick to me." She put her hand on his forehead. "Nope. You're not sick."

He sighed, but he followed her to the barn they used for storage and a garage. He didn't protest when she handed him the hose and rags. As he hooked up the hose, she went inside to get a bucket of soapy water.

"Hi," said her mother, coming into the kitchen from her sewing room. "Getting ready to wash the car?"

"Dylan's going to do it."

"Why him?"

Angel shook her head and frowned at the soapy water. Audrette was right — her mother was spoiling Dylan rotten. "Because he owes me. Because it's his turn. Because he hasn't done anything except mope around since he's been home, while I've done all the chores. He needs to feel useful and like he's a part of this family, Mom."

"That isn't fair, Angelsea. Dylan's been sick."

"Well, he's not sick now. And you don't help him a bit by acting like he is."

"And where did you get all your medical knowledge?" her mother shot back.

She followed Angel to the door. Dylan was nowhere to be seen. "Dill? Where are you?" Angel called, setting down the bucket.

Then she saw something marked in the dust on the side of the car, and she went over to get a better look. "IMPORTANT TEST DIRT. DO NOT WASH," was scrawled from front to back. Just as she burst out laughing, she got a blast of water right in the face. By the time she'd gotten her hands on the hose, she and Dylan were both soaked.

"Quit wasting water!" scolded Gaylon, coming out the door toward them. Angel and Dylan looked at each other only a second before turning the hose on her. A look of shock spread over Gaylon's face as the cold water hit her. Angel put her hand over her mouth. "Oops," she said. Gaylon was soaked from head to toe, and she was heading right for them. Then she saw her mother was grinning as she grabbed for the hose.

It took about twice as long as it should have to wash the car, but the time zipped by. For awhile, they acted like a real family and Angel forgot about Audrette.

— FOURTEEN —

MOM GETS WEIRD

The knock on the door came just as Angel had wrestled the Sunday comics from Dylan.

"Angel — get the door!" yelled her mother from the kitchen.

"OK! Geez! Is everyone else helpless?"

No one bothered to answer. Dylan made a face at her as she got up and tossed the funnies back at him, and Angel knew better than to expect a response from her mother, who was polishing the chrome on the refrigerator.

She had been doing weird things for weeks. She had rearranged the contents of the kitchen cabinets three times and cleaned out all the closets. Even the blades on the ceiling fans were clean. She was also learning French through tapes, and had posted labels on common household objects. The light over the dining room table was "la lumiere." The kitchen clock was "la reveille."

She'd also made mysterious trips to see Romie, whom she'd met before Angel and Audrette fought, and often came home raving about her cornhusk dolls.

In the last few weeks, Gaylon had begun making dried flower arrangements using flowers from her own garden placed in old containers she found at garage sales. Sometimes she made several a day, and Angel was startled one day when she went into the barn and saw more than a dozen lined up against a wall.

When Angel brought one inside to admire, though, her mother turned red, snatched it, and carried it back to the barn. She told Angel and Dylan not to touch them.

"What's next?" Angel muttered as she opened the door, shaking her head.

"Are you shaking your head because it's me?" asked Audrette as Angel opened the door.

"No, of course not. It's my family — they're — never mind." Audrette would've been her first choice of visitors, but the last she would've expected. She pushed the screen door open. "Come on in."

Audrette didn't move. Angel quickly stepped out the door and pulled the door closed. They hadn't spoken since their fight, even though they had seen each other on the bus. Angel had wanted to say something, but she hadn't known how to begin. She wasn't going to lose this opportunity.

"Listen," said Audrette, "can we just pretend we didn't say what we did the other day and start over?"

Angel thought about this for a minute. "No," she said finally, and grabbed Audrette's arm as she turned to go. "Let me finish. See, I can't forget what you said to me. It was all true — every word."

Audrette stood on the porch, arms crossed, looking down, awkwardly shifting her weight from foot to foot.

"But the stuff I said to you, especially the part about us not being friends — I really wish you'd forget about that. I didn't mean it."

Audrette finally looked at her. Her smile was tentative. "I knew you didn't mean it when you said it, but it made me mad anyway. When I got over being mad, I didn't know if I should come over or not."

"I'm glad you did. What made you decide to?"

"You won't believe me if I tell you."

"Try me."

"It was Dylan. At school one day he told me I was the best friend you ever had. And he said he was sorry for being a jerk and he'd try to be better. He and I are OK now, or at least we're trying. We both have awful tempers."

Dylan had been trying. He still griped about chores, but he griped while he did them. He also had stopped trying to get Angel in trouble with their mother.

"I'm sorry I didn't come to your house and apologize, Audrette."

"So why didn't you?"

"Too embarrassed. Afraid you'd slam the door in my face, and I'd look silly."

Audrette grinned.

"So does that mean our deal is on?" asked Angel. "Because we don't have much time to get ready."

"What deal?" Audrette frowned.

"The spring dance. We're still going, right?"

"Angel, I don't like dances. I feel out of place. Look at me — my hair, my clothes. I don't have anything to wear."

"Is that the only thing keeping you from going? You would go if you had something to wear?"

"I guess I'll have to agree or we'll get in another fight," Audrette said grudgingly. "But I'd like to know how either of us is going to get me something to wear. I don't have any money. Do you?"

Angel thought for a moment about the money in the box under her bed and decided not to mention that. "I have a mother who can sew," she said. "She needs something to do, too. Right now she's polishing the refrigerator."

"Does she make your clothes?"

"She didn't before we moved out here, but now she does."

"You always look good. But I'm another story. I don't think anyone can fix me."

"That's silly, Audrette. Nothing needs fixing. Well, maybe your hair. Anyway, let's go talk to Mom about it."

"No! Why would your mom want to make me a dress? Maybe this isn't a good idea."

"It's a great idea. Look, you don't have to come in right now if you don't want to. I'll ask her. I know she'll do it. We'll talk more about it tomorrow."

Audrette was backing away, but she nodded. She wasn't enthusiastic, but at least she wasn't saying no.

"Thanks for coming over," Angel said, but Audrette was jogging away. Angel didn't know whether she had heard or not until Audrette's arm shot up in a goodbye wave.

Dylan glanced up but quickly looked away when Angel came in. She started to say something to him, but her mother interrupted.

"Who was that?" she called from the kitchen.

"Later, you," Angel said to Dylan, who ignored her. She walked into the kitchen. Her mother was folding cup towels which she had just ironed. Angel resisted the temptation to roll her eyes.

"It was Audrette. We talked about going to the spring dance. The thing is, Audrette doesn't own a dress. Can you believe that?"

"I've never seen her wear anything but those old baggy jeans," said Gaylon, distracted. "I don't guess any of your dresses would fit her?"

"I'm too tall, Mom. And she can't afford to buy a dress. But I bet someone could make her one that wouldn't cost much."

"That's probably true," said Gaylon.

"You, for example."

Her mother stopped folding and stared. "I guess I could. I would rather make you a dress, though, since I know how to fit you better."

This wasn't the time to tell her mom she was going to buy a new dress. She'd have to figure out how to do that later. "I already have something to wear. My pink print."

"That's very unselfish of you, Angel," said Gaylon. "All right — I'll do it. But I need to start right away. We can shop for fabric tomorrow since I have an appointment in town anyway. I'll pick you up after school. Be sure to tell Audrette so she can come with us and pick out the fabric."

But Angel decided not to tell Audrette. She believed she and her mother could more easily pick out something that would look good. Frankly, she worried about Audrette's taste.

She was surprised at how pretty her mother looked when she arrived at school to pick her up. She always looked good in her red suit, but she looked even better than usual. She had dried her hair instead of just pulling it back, and she wore red earrings. Her skin glowed. She also had on her black patent-leather pumps. Angel hadn't seen her in anything but jeans for months.

"Why are you so dressed up?" Angel asked curiously.

"I told you, I had an appointment. Where's Audrette?"

"I want to surprise her."

"Angel, you didn't tell her? She should pick out her own dress pattern, at least."

"We can find something nice for her, Mom. We have good taste."

Gaylon shook her head but didn't argue. Angel wanted to ask what the appointment was, but she sensed she shouldn't. They shopped almost without talking, choosing a simple pattern for a one-piece dress with cap sleeves, belted waist, and a softly shirred skirt. Next they found a silky fabric in mint green that Angel's mother said would look good with Audrette's fair skin and reddish hair. It was on sale. Her mother hadn't said anything about money, but Angel could tell she was relieved at the price.

When they got back to the car, her mother put the key into the ignition, but didn't turn it on. She just sat there, staring at the steering wheel.

"Mom? What's up?"

"Angelsea," began Gaylon, "I have something to tell you. Dylan, too. But I want to tell you first. If you know before he does, I think it will be easier for me to tell him. Maybe you can help me figure out how. It's about the appointment I had today in town."

Angel looked at her mom, her heart pounding. This was going to be bad. Her mom must have decided to get a divorce, or maybe her father had. She tried to swallow, but couldn't. She felt like she was suffocating.

She rolled down the window quickly, scraping her knuckles on the inside of the door.

"The thing is," her mother said, "I can't go on doing what I'm doing. Angel, are you all right?"

"Just tell me when you're going to do it, so I'll be prepared."

"I don't know just yet," her mother said, her voice suddenly filled with doubt. "If I had known it would bother you so much, I wouldn't have even considered it. But I don't have to decide today. I've got a few days. I'll certainly have time to make Audrette's dress. And we all will have time to talk about it. I know it's important to you to talk about things, to be involved in what's going on."

"Yeah, like I have a part in this decision," Angel snorted. "Just go ahead and do it. What does it matter what Dylan and I think? Just don't you and Dad fight over everything, OK? Don't do that to Dylan and me."

"Why should your dad care? It makes no difference to him. It's you I'm concerned about. I guess I should have said something to you before I went to the interview. But since the job is only part time, I thought you probably wouldn't care. We could use the money, especially if we buy the house. Your father is good about expenses, but I feel bad with him bearing most of the burden. Does my working now and then bother you that much?"

Angel sucked in her breath. She felt stupid as she

turned to look at her mother. Suddenly, understanding flooded Gaylon's face.

"For heaven's sake! You thought I was talking about getting a divorce!"

Angel nodded.

"Oh, Angel, I'm sorry! Believe it or not, your father and I haven't talked about divorce. If we do, you and Dylan will be involved in that discussion. But it's premature."

Angel tried to smile, but she felt silly. Gaylon started the car.

"The job is at the Floral Craft Gallery. They'll actually be teaching me how to dry my flowers and how to make arrangements. And they might buy the ones I've already made — they bought the one I took with me to the interview. Anyway, if I do it, you and Dylan would have to do more around the house, and there would be fewer homemade meals."

Angel was so relieved she wouldn't have minded if her mother said she would have to cook all the meals. "It's all right, Mom. You should do it, if you want to. You're good at it, although I'm not sure you need lessons. You're a natural."

Her mother studied her for a moment.

"What?" asked Angel.

"Oh, nothing much. I was just thinking how unselfish you've been."

Angel suddenly thought about the money she had held back, and what her mother had just paid for

Audrette's pattern and fabric. She could have paid for it with her own money.

"Mom," she began. Gaylon looked at her expectantly. "Nothing. Never mind." She told herself she didn't know how to begin.

Gaylon told Dylan about the job when they got home.

"Will I get more allowance if I do more chores?" he asked. "I want to buy a new basketball."

"No. And don't pitch such a fit at my impending absence," said Gaylon, heading for the kitchen. "You'll make me feel guilty."

Angel hadn't spoken to Dylan yet about Audrette. As he reclined on the floor in front of the television, she nudged him in the ribs with her foot.

"You been pokin' around in my business, little brother?"

"What do you mean?"

"Oh, Audrette told me about something you said to her. Something about me being unbearable."

"You're always unbearable. Always were, still are." He grinned.

"Oh yeah? Well, I don't like to give you a big head, but I appreciate what you did. Even if you are a busybody."

"I didn't do anything. And don't go spreading it around that I'm a nice guy."

"Who'd believe me anyway?"

—FIFTEEN—

THE THEFT

Gaylon took the job right after she started on Audrette's dress, and suddenly there was calmness at home. There was also more money, since the gallery bought her arrangements, but they still had to be careful.

Dylan was getting better all the time. He was even getting back to his science experiments, which Angel discovered when she found the milk carton full of something that looked like ants frozen in liquid in the big chest freezer.

"Dylan," she said, holding up the carton, "is this yours?"

"Put it back before you ruin everything!" he said, running to snatch it out of her hands.

She held it just out of his reach.

She pretended to drop it, then felt awful as his face went white, and gently replaced it in the freezer.

"It looks like frozen ants," she said. "What is it?"

"Frozen ants."

She stared at him, and he finally gave in. "I made a special solution and suspended them in it to see if they'd come back to life when they're thawed."

"What's in the special solution?"

He shrugged. "Soap and stuff."

"When do they come out?"

"I haven't figured that out yet."

She tried to hide her smile because she didn't want Dylan to think she was laughing at him. She was just glad he was back to experimenting.

These days Angel's worries were for her parents and what would become of them. Before she took the job, Gaylon had eaten lunch with Gary in town once each week and talked to him several times by phone. Now, something had to give, and Angel sensed it was the lunch and phone calls.

"Do you ever see Dad any more?" Angel asked her mother one day after school.

If her mother was surprised, she gave no sign. She sat at the kitchen table, basting a facing on Audrette's dress. She glanced at Angel and removed the pins from her mouth.

"Sometimes. We still have lunch now and then. Why?"

"But you never go to town any more just to see him."

"That's true. I have a lot more to do now. Besides, I get tired of doing all the driving."

"What do you mean?"

"That the road between here and town works both ways. Your father could come out here more. How many times has he been here since we moved?"

"Not many," Angel admitted. She was filling a glass with ice. Dylan was at the kitchen table, sketching a picture of something. They both pretended to concentrate on what they were doing, but his pencil had stopped. Gaylon glanced at Dylan, then at Angel, then put Audrette's dress on the table.

"Let's talk," she said. "You two must have questions. Let's say for ten minutes you get to ask anything you want to."

Angel hesitated, glancing at Dylan before she asked, "Do you think Dad feels welcome out here?"

"I think so, although maybe I should make that perfectly clear."

"Do you think he will ever move in with us?"

"He's still thinking about it, but he's never said one way or the other. Only he can say for sure, and he may not even know yet."

"Would you want him to?" asked Dylan.

"I'd give it a try. I just don't want to go back to the way things were."

"Neither do I," said Angel, surprising herself.

"Me neither," Dylan said, surprising everyone.

"Then it's unanimous," said Gaylon. "What else?"

"How could you be sure you wouldn't fight anymore?" Dylan asked.

"I can't be sure. All couples have disagreements. What we would want to do is make sure they didn't get out of hand like before. But I think many of the reasons we fought have disappeared."

"They have?" asked Angel. "So is divorce out of the picture? Or are we going to live like this — sort of divorced — forever? And what if Dylan or I, or both of us, wanted to live with Dad?"

Her mother's face turned red. "Well, your first question first. We haven't talked about divorce, but I wouldn't say it's out of the picture. It's just never been in the picture. I wasn't lying when I told you that before, Angel. But to be very honest, I don't think we would talk about it all that much. I think one of us would decide, and tell the other one, and that would be that.

"As for your second question — I can't tell you how much longer we will live apart. It might be forever." She paused, staring at Audrette's dress. "You are both old enough to make your own decisions about where you live. That's my mature response. My honest and childish answer is that I couldn't stand to live without either of you, and if you decided to live with your father, I'd probably lock you in your rooms. Having you leave for college is going to be hard enough."

They were all silent a moment. "Any more questions?" Gaylon asked them.

Angel shook her head. "Not from me. But can we do this again sometime?"

"Anytime. And we could've talked longer. I thought the ten-minute limit would give you a push."

The next morning before school, Angel's mother called her into the sewing room. She was holding Audrette's dress, pressed crisply, on a hanger. "Except for the hem, I finished it last night," Gaylon said.

"It's beautiful," said Angel, gaping. "Even more than I thought it would be."

"She'll need to try it on. You want to take it to school today? Be sure and mark where the hem should go with this piece of chalk, and if there's a spot that doesn't fit right, she needs to come over here and try it on so I can fix it."

Angel hurried through breakfast, anxious to get on the school bus, anxious to show Audrette her dress. She presented it to her in a shopping bag.

Audrette's eyes got big as she looked into the bag, bigger still when she pulled out the dress. "It's gorgeous," she breathed. "I thought your mother said no and you just didn't want to tell me." She looked almost worshipful. Angel squirmed in her seat.

"You picked this out, didn't you?" Audrette asked.

"I helped. I picked out the pattern, and Mom chose the material. She said the color would bring out the warm tones in your skin. I hope you don't mind us picking everything."

"No, I don't mind. I guess I might if I knew anything about clothes. But I wouldn't have even known where to start. I'm glad you picked it out."

In a flash, Angel remembered how unimportant she felt the day her mother told her they were moving to Crookwood to a house she had never seen. She realized she had done the same thing to Audrette. She touched her friend's arm.

"I'm sorry, Audrette. My mother said you should go with us, and she was right. I just thought I could do a better job."

"I might be mad if it weren't so beautiful," Audrette said.

Angel felt better as she watched Audrette inspect the dress inside and out. "Your mom did all this? How'd she learn?"

"Same way you learned to cut hair, I guess. Anyway, all it needs is a hem, and you need to try it on today so I can mark where. We could do that at my house, right after school, if you have time."

"I can't. Gram wants me home to help her in the garden before it gets dark. Could we do it at lunch?"

They agreed to meet in the locker room at noon. Everyone else would be eating and they'd have the place to themselves. But when Angel got there a few minutes after twelve, she found Audrette hunched over in the corner, sobbing. The sight made the hair on the back of her neck stand up.

"What's the matter?" she asked, sinking down beside her friend.

Audrette was sobbing much too hard to speak. Finally, she choked out, "Gone! Stolen!"

Angel looked around. There was nothing on the bench except books. No shopping bag, no green dress. Her heart pounded. "Audrette, did someone take your dress?"

Audrette nodded, sobbing harder.

"Didn't you lock it in your locker?"

She shrugged, then unclenched her right fist, which she had been holding at her side. She'd been clutching the padlock so tightly it had turned her palm an angry red. "I thought I locked it, but it was open when I got here!" she said through sobs.

Angel took the padlock and inspected it. There were scratch marks on the bottom near the keyhole. Someone had picked it. As the full impact of what had happened hit her, she expected to be angry. But she was calm. She knew exactly what she was going to do. It felt good to have a plan. She held Audrette's hand and stroked her hair.

The sobs finally lessened, then stopped. Audrette blew her nose a couple of times, walked to the sink, and washed her face. She didn't look at Angel until she sat down again.

"What are we going to do? What do we tell your mother? That's the nicest thing anyone's ever given me," she said, her eyes filling again.

"We tell her what happened. This is a real compliment to her sewing talents."

Audrette sighed, brushed away the new tears, and looked at the floor.

"I wasn't meant to go to the dance, Angel."

"That's silly. You're going. Never mind the details. We'll figure it out. Let's go eat lunch."

They weren't much company for each other. Angel was too preoccupied, and Audrette kept saying how stupid she was not to have locked the dress up. Finally Angel said, "You did lock it. You wouldn't forget something like that. Didn't you see the scratches on the bottom of the lock?"

Audrette nodded. "But how can you be sure I didn't make them with my key?"

"I just know," Angel said with a shrug. "I'll bet you a dollar the lock doesn't work very well anymore."

"I don't have a dollar," Audrette said dully. "And I'd rather not know."

For the rest of the day, through all her classes, Angel couldn't think about anything else but what they were going to do next. She wanted to tell Audrette, but she had to wait for the right time. There was a theft she'd have to get over first. She took one look at her face when they boarded the school bus and knew that it still wasn't time.

"Shall I tell you jokes?" Angel asked her.

"I know you're just trying to make me feel better, but I'd rather not talk. I just feel kind of rotten. And

I'd like to savor that feeling for awhile. I'm good at it."

"Audrette —"

"I mean it, Angel. I don't want any 'You'll feel better tomorrow' lines. Right now I want to feel lousy."

"OK, I'll be quiet," said Angel.

Once home, Angel ran upstairs, reached under the bed and grabbed her money box. She took off the lid carefully, as if the contents were made of fragile glass, and counted one more time. Sixty dollars. There had been seventy-five cents in there, too, but she had taken that yesterday to have some extra change. Sixty dollars would buy a nice dress.

"Angel!" her mother called up the stairs. "I need help with dinner!"

As she walked downstairs, Angel tried to think of a way to tell her mother the dress had been stolen. She decided to be direct.

"Mom — about the dress..."

"Yes. I've been waiting to hear. What did Audrette think?"

"She said it was gorgeous. And it was."

"And did it fit?"

Angel was silent.

"You can tell me if it didn't. Dresses can always be altered. Shouldn't be too hard. Was it too small or too big? Too big, I'll bet. She's pretty small."

"I don't know, Mom. Someone stole it from Audrette's locker before she could try it on." She looked at her mother, searching her face. Their eyes locked for a moment then Gaylon looked away.

"I hope they do a good job on the hem," she said, her voice calm. "You have any idea who'd do such a thing?"

Angel had lots of ideas, but didn't want to say them out loud. "I'm not sure," she said, looking at her mother.

Neither of them spoke for almost five minutes. Then Gaylon said, "I don't have a lot of time, but I could make another dress."

This was tempting. Gaylon was fast and accomplished with a needle and thread, and a handmade dress might fit Audrette even better than one they could buy. But as Angel rolled the idea around in her head, she felt ashamed. It would cost her mother several nights of staying up late, if not all night, to finish.

"No, Mom. But there is something you can do — take Audrette and me shopping after school one day this week? I'm going to buy her a dress." She said it casually as she sliced yellow squash for a casserole.

"How are you going to buy her a dress?"

"I have some money saved."

Silence descended on them like a fog. The only sounds were Angel's knife clicking on the cutting board and the clock ticking off seconds. Angel counted to ten before her mother's question came: "Where did you get the money?" Gaylon, who had been putting pork chops in hot oil, stood with a chop in each hand, as she turned to look at her daughter.

The knife blade clicked, the clock ticked. "Been saving it. From money I had before we moved, and from what you and Dad have been giving me."

"For what?" her mother asked, dropping the chops into the oil. She paused, then said, "You were saving that money to buy your own dress, weren't you?"

Afraid her face would give her away Angel made sure to keep her head down. "I'm wearing my pink print. I don't need another dress."

"It's all right to want something new, Angel."

Just then Dylan came in with a homework question. Angel was glad she didn't have to talk about the dress any more. Now all she had to do was convince Audrette. It would probably be easier to talk Dylan into wearing a skirt.

—— SIXTEEN ——

G O I N G   S H O P P I N G

Audrette looked almost like herself when she got on the bus the next morning.

"Can I talk today?" Angel asked her.

"Depends on what you talk about. If you talk about something interesting, you have my undivided attention."

"This is interesting, I promise. You are going shopping with Mom and me one day after school to buy you a dress."

Audrette plopped down. "I changed my mind. No talking. And by the way, I've never even been inside a store that sells dresses."

"Time you went. Give me one good reason not to go."

"I don't have any money." Audrette busied herself pulling books out of her bag.

"We will have enough money to buy a great dress."

"Fine. Buy yourself a great dress."

"So you'll want to figure out which day is good so your Gram will know you'll be late," continued Angel, as if Audrette hadn't said anything. "We'll drop you home afterward. Just tell her you have to go to town with Mom and me. You don't have to say what it's for. Unless you want to. Or you can ask her to come, too."

"Oh, I'm sure all of that will make a big difference. Listen, Angel, if Gram wants me home, it doesn't matter if the White House has invited me to high tea. Besides, I already told you I'm not going."

"We're going to buy you a dress, Audrette. You're going. I hope we can find a green one, the same color as the one Mom made you." She glanced at Audrette, whose chin was jutting out stubbornly. "I'm not letting you out of our deal. You said you'd go to the dance, and you're going."

Neither of them spoke for awhile. Then Audrette asked, "How did your mother take the news?"

"She was mad. She wanted to know if I had an idea who stole it."

"Do you?"

"Yes. Do you?"

"Yes," sighed Audrette. "Horrible, isn't it? But I can't help it. I won't tell you who I think did it if you won't tell me who you think did it. Deal?"

Angel nodded. Each time she got a picture of the person stealing it, a lump that felt like lead formed in her stomach.

Audrette sighed again. "I've never tried on clothes before. Don't they expect you to buy it if you try it on?"

"You will be going with an expert, and you will be surprised at how easy and fun shopping is. There aren't any rules. I've tried on tons of clothes I've never bought. They want you to like what you buy."

"But most of all, they want you to buy, right? Don't they pressure you?"

"Remember, my mom is going. They don't treat you like a leper so much when there's an adult with you."

Audrette was silent for a minute. "All right. I'll do it on one condition. You have to let me pay you back. Somehow. And I think I know how."

"All right. How?"

"That will be my secret."

"All right. You pay me back. Whenever. So you'll go?"

Audrette nodded unenthusiastically, but Angel knew the deal was on. She always did what she said she'd do. They decided on the next day for the shopping trip, and Gaylon was right on time after school. "Hi, Audrette," she said. "I'm so sorry someone stole your dress."

"I should be apologizing to you, Mrs. Mead. If I hadn't been so careless…"

Gaylon waved her hand. "It wasn't your fault. Whoever wanted it would've found a way to get it no matter what. Thieves always do."

Audrette smiled, relieved. And finally she looked excited.

Once in the store, Amanda's Closet, Angel headed straight for the sale rack, which had always been in the back. She was pleased to see it was crammed full of dresses. She glanced from the rack to Audrette, and went to the fives.

"Wow, look at these!" she said. "Two outfits to start with!" One was a light green dress with tiny white dots. The second was a set, a mint-green blouse with small pearl buttons, and a skirt with small green, yellow and red flowers on a mint green background.

"What do you think?" she asked, thrusting the green blouse under Audrette's chin.

"I don't know, Angel. How does it look? Mrs. Mead?"

"I think this is great," Angel said, shaking the green blouse and skirt.

"But you should try both," said Gaylon. "And we'll wait right here, so come show us."

Angel pointed Audrette to the dressing room. She tried on the dress first. The waist was too short and the skirt too long. Angel and her mother both shook their heads as she emerged. Audrette looked relieved and hurried back to the dressing room.

Angel and her mother were looking at pants when someone behind them spoke their names.

"Angelsea...Mrs. Mead...what a surprise."

Angel knew without turning around it was Cat. She considered pretending she hadn't heard, since she hadn't spoken to Cat since the pregnancy rumor. But her mother was already replying. "Catherine, it's been months! How have you been? And how is your mother?"

Angel turned around to see Cat dressed in a while blouse and khaki shorts, and enough gold jewelry to impress Fort Knox.

As they were exchanging meaningless pleasantries, Angel noticed that something behind her had caught Cat's attention. It was Audrette wearing the skirt and blouse.

"How's this look?" Audrette asked them.

"Lovely," said Gaylon.

Angel made a circle with her thumb and forefinger. The blouse fit perfectly, with the cap sleeves showing off Audrette's toned, tan arms. The fit of the skirt emphasized her slimness. It was just right.

"I've got to be going," Cat said quickly. "I'm meeting someone."

Angel waved without looking up as she brushed imaginary wrinkles off Audrette's skirt. "What do you think, Mom?" Angel pointed to Audrette.

"I'm with you," she said, smiling.

"What do you think, Audrette? You like this one?"

Audrette nodded, her eyes fixed on the store exit. Angel knew she was watching Cat leave.

"Wasn't that a friend of yours?" she asked.

Angel shrugged. "A long time ago." She was surprised at how easily she said it. It sounded natural.

"I'm going to change now," said Audrette.

She disappeared into the dressing room. Angel and her mother looked at each other.

"I think you did quite well today," said Gaylon.

Angel nodded. "Yes. I think so, too."

"Geez," said Dylan when they came out of the store, "what did you say to Cat? She saw me, but she looked right through me. Didn't even say hello."

"Hi and 'bye," replied Angel, shrugging.

"I thought we had a pleasant visit," said her mother.

As they passed a pizza bar, Angel heard a shriek of laughter. She turned to see Cat and some other girls sitting in a back booth, doubled over with giggles. Everyone was staring at them. Angel was relieved she wasn't with them.

——SEVENTEEN——

A U D R E T T E ' S   S U R P R I S E

"Not bad, Angelsea Mead. Not even a little bit."

She patted her hair and looked at herself from the right, left, and back. She was surprised at how good her pink print dress looked. She bought it a year ago for a party at Cat's, and it had been out of her closet only once since then, for the move to Crookwood. It still fit, which meant that she hadn't gotten any taller. That was a relief.

"Hair looks good, too," she said to the girl in the mirror.

The sound of her own voice gave Angel confidence, which was good since she was on her way to a dance without a date in a dress she had worn before. There was a soft tap on her door, and her mother came in. She handed Angel a small package wrapped in blue foil paper.

"It isn't much, but I wanted you to go to your dance wearing at least one new thing."

Angel tore open the paper and pulled out an expensive lipstick.

"New shade," said her mother. "I saw it and thought it was your color."

She was right about the color. It wasn't one of those baby-pinks that you could hardly see, but somewhere between pink and hot pink, called Bright Berry. Angel slid it over her lips, the color immediately emphasizing the tint in her cheeks.

"Very nice," her mother said approvingly. "Listen, Audrette isn't going to walk over, is she?"

"She said Romie would bring her."

"I didn't know Romie drove."

"She doesn't, much. I guess she thought this was a special occasion."

As Angel examined herself, a horrible thought came to mind. What about Audrette's shoes? Her work boots were the only shoes she ever wore. She looked down at her own feet.

"What's the matter? You look like you just heard some awful news," her mother said.

"Oh, nothing. I just wondered what shoes Audrette was wearing."

"Everything will be fine, I'm sure." Her mother turned to go. "Come down and model for Dylan and me. We don't get to see you like this very often. Your brother could use some culture."

Relieved when her mother left, Angel took one more peek in the mirror and smiled. A tall, attractive brunette with a stylish haircut and just-right makeup smiled back. She wished the version in the mirror could go without her. She, at least, appeared calm and confident.

She and Audrette would be two oddballs amidst the couples. She hoped no one was standing outside to see her mother drop them off or pick them up.

"Get used to it," she told the girl in the mirror. "Because you're not going to get a car anytime soon and who's going to drive out here for a date? No money and nowhere to go, even if you did have a car." She made a face at the girl in the mirror.

"Angel!" Her mother was calling to her up the stairs. "There's a car coming up the drive. I'm sure it's Audrette and Romie."

Angel's stomach somersaulted. "I don't want to go to this stupid dance," she said to the girl in the mirror, who stared back, big-eyed. Her face was pale now instead of pink. Why had she insisted they do this? She and Audrette could be camped out in front of the TV right now, with a bowl of popcorn between them, watching a movie, merely wishing they had gone. "Angel!"

"I'm coming!"

As she reached the stairs, she was irritated to see Dylan peeking out the window as her mother answered the door. "Geez," she muttered. "I'm glad it's only Romie and Audrette, and not a real date. You'd think we were hillbillies."

She suddenly stopped on the stairs, mouth agape, staring at the open doorway. In the middle of it stood a vision in a mint-green blouse and flowered skirt. Auburn hair cascaded in waves around her face, softening the glasses she wore and making her eyes appear even more blue. On her feet were dainty green sandals. And was the vision wearing lipstick? "Wow!" was all Angel could say.

Audrette didn't hear her, though. She was looking behind her and motioning to someone. Angel wondered why Romie needed to come inside. She hoped she wasn't planning to stay.

But it wasn't Romie who walked in behind Audrette. It was a tall male wearing a crisp shirt, tie and sports jacket and carrying a corsage box. As Audrette looked up at Angel on the stairway and pointed, his eyes followed and he smiled. Angel froze, knowing that she would stumble and fall if she took another step. Audrette had just led Clifton Neal through her doorway.

"Are you going to come down soon," Audrette said, "or should we come join you? I want you to meet my cousin, Clifton Neal. He's brought you a corsage — see mine?" She held up her wrist to show off a bouquet of mint-green carnations. She turned to Angel's mother. "Cliff is going to take us to the dance, if that's all right. He's a good driver — never had a ticket, right Cliff?"

As her mother and Audrette discussed when they'd be home, Angel negotiated the stairs, praying she would not fall. She kept her eyes glued to the floor, afraid to look at the handsome guy standing in her entryway. Was he really there, or was this a dream?

"Well, finally, you decide to come down!" Audrette cried. "Cliff, this is my very best friend in the world — besides my Gram, of course, and I guess I technically can't count her as a friend — Angelsea Mead. Isn't that a neat name? Get her to tell you where she got it. The given name, I mean, you know where she got the last name. From her father, of course. He's not here right now, but that's another story."

"We've met — sort of," muttered Clifton, but Audrette paid no attention.

"Anyhow, Angel — that's short for Angelsea — and her mother are responsible for this outfit I'm wearing. Oh, Angel, did you see my shoes? Gram bought them for me. I picked them out, but she bought them. In fact, she's the one who reminded me I would need some. She was more excited about this than I was. Do you think they're all right?"

"What?" Angel said.

"What what?" said Audrette.

"Do I think what are all right?" Angel replied, exasperated. She felt as if she had shrunk, as Clifton Neal was much taller than she was. Or maybe she was melting. Her underarms were certainly damp enough.

159

"The shoes, of course. Gosh, Angel, have you been asleep or something? You act like you're in a trance!"

Angel wanted to snap that Audrette was chattering like she was plugged into electricity, but she didn't want to say that in front of Clifton Neal. Was his hair really that blond, or was it just the light?

"The shoes are fine."

"You look lovely, Audrette," Gaylon said. She turned to Clifton Neal. "I'm Gaylon Mead, Angel's mother, and this is Dylan, my son. Do you want me to pin that corsage on Angel?"

He looked relieved as he handed the box to her.

"Boy, you look great, Angel. Doesn't she look great, Cliff? Of course Angel always looks great. You know Angel's probably the prettiest girl in her class. And smart, too. And she has a green thumb. You should see her garden. It's her mother's, too, but Angel helped. Maybe you could come over here sometime in the daylight and see it. I'm sure Angel would be glad to show it to you."

Angel felt her face get hot. As her mother pinned the flower — a fragrant pink rose — on the shoulder of her dress, she put her hand on Angel's forehead. "Do you feel all right, dear? You look flushed."

She thanked her mother silently for calling attention to her red face, and considered announcing that she was sick and would spend the evening in bed. It sounded dramatic and it would certainly serve Audrette right for springing this surprise on her. Were

Clifton Neal's eyes blue or gray? Blue, she thought, but in this light she could not be sure.

"I'm fine, just fine," she replied to her mother in a low voice. She turned to Audrette. "We should go." As her mother gave final instructions to Clifton about safe driving and curfew, she grabbed Audrette's arm and yanked her onto the porch.

"Why don't you just put a blinking sign on me: 'Needs a date'?" she hissed, glancing back to make sure her mother still had Clifton cornered. "What's the matter with you anyway? You sound like a windup talking doll!"

"I'm sorry, Angel, I'm just nervous. I'll be good, I promise. Anyhow, aren't you surprised? I was just busting to tell you Clifton Neal was my cousin, but I wanted to surprise you. Remember when I told you I'd pay you back for the dress somehow? I thought getting him to take us to the dance would be the best surprise I could put together."

"File this away for future reference, OK? Sometimes I don't like to be surprised...like when you're going to bring someone to my house who I...sort of...like. Omigod! You didn't tell him that, did you?"

"Well, no, of course not. I'm not a blabbermouth." She glanced at Angel's face. "OK, I am a blabbermouth, but a selective one. I didn't tell him you had a thing for him. I just asked him if he'd take me and a friend to the dance, and he asked me who the friend was, and I told him you. And he said yes."

"Just like that, huh?" said Angel, snapping her fingers.

"Pretty much. I did have to promise to wash his car a couple of times."

Angel hit her forehead with her fist. She felt like the frumpy blind date of a hired escort. "Gee, is that all?" she said, glaring at Audrette. "You mean you didn't throw in a wax job, too? Why don't we just pool our money and buy him a new car? A Jag or something?"

"I don't see why you're so snippy. You look beautiful, and you're going to the dance with the handsomest boy in the senior class. He's nice, too, and you like him. What's the big deal if I had to do something extra to get him to take us? It's not like you have to wash his car. Besides, I did this for you."

"Shush! Here he comes. See if you can get that mouth in control before you tell him my shoe size." She pressed her lips together and flicked her hand across her lips as if she were zipping them shut.

When Clifton Neal asked who wanted to sit up front, Angel shot Audrette a warning look. "I'll sit in back," she said.

The silence she'd wished for was heavy with awkwardness. Miserable, she played with her ring in the dark and tried frantically to think of something clever to say. Suddenly she blurted, "Nice car!" Clifton jumped at the unexpected sound of her voice, and Audrette turned to look at her. Angel wondered if they were going slow enough for her to jump out.

"Thanks," Clifton said finally, glancing at her in the rearview mirror.

More silence. Angel started to panic. The whole night couldn't be like this, could it? She sensed that Audrette was about to burst. She probably couldn't hold her tongue much longer.

"So how did you get your name?" Clifton asked. It was Angel's turn to jump.

"What?"

"Audrette said there was a story behind your name. What's the story?"

"Oh, it's really nothing. My parents just named me after a song."

"Boy!" exploded Audrette. "Do you know how to make an interesting story dull! I'll remember that sometime when I have insomnia. Anyhow, Cliff, here's the deal."

As Audrette jabbered on, Angel leaned back against the car seat, grateful that the car was dark so no one could see her face. She was sure her makeup had come off. She wished Clifton would turn the car around and take her home.

"Now, isn't that how it happened?" Audrette said, turning to Angel for confirmation.

"What? Oh, yes, I guess so."

"So what did you do with the plaque?" Clifton asked. "You know," he said, when Angel didn't answer, "the one with the song on it? I'd like to see it sometime."

"I'm sure she would show it to you," volunteered Audrette. "Wouldn't you, Angel?"

"I think my dad has it and he...he doesn't live with us."

Clifton looked at her in the mirror again. "Oh," he said. "I'm sorry."

Feeling awful, Angel looked away. She didn't know why she'd felt compelled to say that, but she was sure he didn't want to have anything to do with her now.

Getting to the dance took a year. No parking places were nearby, so Clifton let the two girls out at the door and went off to park the car.

"I'll be surprised if he comes back," said Angel. "He probably decided to go somewhere else. We'll just be standing here looking like idiots."

Audrette regarded Angel solemnly. "You're acting like an idiot, so maybe you deserve to be left. But you know what? I'm going to have a good time if it kills me. And if you don't loosen up and start acting like the Angelsea Mead I know, we may both leave you."

She was right. Audrette hadn't done anything wrong. In fact, she had done something very thoughtful. She was about to apologize when Clifton reappeared. He smiled at both of them — were his teeth really that white? — and held out an arm on each side.

"Shall we?"

Angel was filled with determination that this would be a special night, for Audrette as well as for her. "Yes," she said, taking Audrette's right arm and placing it through Clifton's left. She hooked his other arm inside hers. "We don't want to miss any of the action."

BARBARA ELMORE

── EIGHTEEN ──

A GOOD TIME WAS HAD

"It was your big idea to come. What are we going to do now?" Audrette said.

She and Angel sat at a table by themselves. Clifton had drifted away, and stood in a group of boys at the edge of the dance floor. He fit right in, Angel noted. They all looked bored, too.

Angel had overlooked one thing in her plan to go to the dance. Actually, she hadn't known it. Neither Audrette nor Clifton knew how to dance.

Except for that, Clifton had been very nice, exactly what Angel had hoped he would be like. He had asked how she liked her new home, and if she enjoyed living in the country. He had talked about movies and where he was going to college next year.

But after awhile, he had left them. It was clear he didn't want to be at the dance. Nor did Audrette.

"Did you hear me?" she demanded, scattering Angel's thoughts. "What are we going to do now?"

"I haven't figured it out yet," Angel replied. "If you'll hush, though, and let me think, I'll come up with something."

"Angel, let's just go! Neither of us is having fun, and look at Cliff. He looks like he's sleepwalking!"

Angel looked at her, thinking. "All right. I've got an idea. Go get him and I'll wait outside."

Audrette hesitated only a moment. Angel watched at the door to make sure she went over to the group of boys before she went outside to wait. This was a gamble, but she was counting on them liking to do the same kinds of things she liked. Other than dancing.

Audrette and Clifton both looked wary as they joined her.

"You two want to do something else?" Angel asked them in the most confident voice she could muster. They nodded. She asked Clifton to get the car.

"Where are we going?" Audrette asked as they waited for him.

"You'll see."

"Why won't you tell me? What if I don't like where we're going?"

"You'll love it, and we'll be the best-dressed people there."

Angel took the front seat this time, directing Clifton down familiar San Marcos streets, hoping he wouldn't realize too soon where they were going. In a few minutes, they pulled up at San Marcos Putt-O-Rama.

"Putt-putt!" cried Audrette. "I always wanted to play!"

"You mean you never have?" said Angel. "Well, it's time you did."

They played for hours, until their pooled funds ran out. The manager even gave them a free game because they were having so much fun and because they were all dressed up. Angel beat the others at almost every obstacle. Audrette ran a close third behind Clifton.

"You're good at this," said Clifton. "What other games do you play?"

"Just about anything my brother does. He's a natural athlete, and he always needed a partner. Dad wasn't home much."

"Hey, what about me?" demanded Audrette. "This is only my first time."

"You've got to be kidding!" said Angel. "It took me a dozen times to get where you are."

"Sorry to say it, guys, but the money is gone and it's early." Clifton said. "So what now?

Angel invited them back to her house. "My mom's cool — she'll leave us alone. Now my brother is another matter."

"That'd be good," said Clifton. "I like your house. It felt like home."

"And we can stay up later because we're already there. I'm spending the night at Angel's," she told Cliff.

They all were talking so much the drive to Crookwood was the shortest in Angel's memory. When they pulled up at the house, they noticed someone on the darkened front porch scrambling to escape from the headlights.

"Who is that?" asked Clifton, as he pulled up and turned off his lights.

Angel was pretty sure, but she didn't say anything until, her eyes grown accustomed to the darkness, she recognized the figure on the porch. "Dylan, is that you and your hot dog contraption?" she called, getting out of the car. This was an invention he often used outside because he didn't want Gaylon to know about it.

"Yes," came the guilty-sounding voice.

"How many have you done?" she asked, walking to the porch.

"Only two. You going to tell Mom?"

"Depends. You have any more?" He nodded. She turned around to Clifton and Audrette, who had followed her. "Who wants an electric hot dog? That is, if I can find some buns."

"We have buns," said Dylan. "A whole package. I haven't even opened them yet. I've been eating the weenies without the buns."

Everyone wanted at least one, so she told Dylan to bring his contraption inside and demonstrate how it worked.

"But what about Mom?" he asked.

"You think she doesn't know?" He seemed relieved but also disappointed, so she didn't tell him that Gaylon knew about most of his secret inventions.

Dylan's eagerness to show off his latest invention overcame any reluctance. He carried it into the kitchen under his arm and gently placed it on the kitchen table. It was a flat, rectangular piece of wood with two nails hammered through it side-by-side. The nails were the width of a wiener. Around each nail's head, Dylan had left enough space to wrap the wire of an electrical cord he had gotten from an old lamp, still attached to the plug.

"See," said Dylan, demonstrating, "you punch a couple of holes in a hot dog with a fork. Then you put it here." He skewered the wiener on the two nails, close to the tips. "Then you plug it in, and zap!" In moments the hot dog sizzled and popped. "Ready!" cried Dylan.

Angel was standing by with buns she had heated in the microwave. On the table, she had put ketchup, mustard and relish. "Douse 'em good," she said. "Dylan's invention is ingenious, but the dogs taste like electricity."

"What does electricity taste like?" Clifton asked, clearly fascinated.

"You'll see," said Angel. "It's why we always have popcorn and chips and stuff, too," she added, pulling bags of chips and microwave popcorn out of the pantry.

Soon they had a party, with the four of them gobbling everything in sight and Dylan telling about his inventions and what led to each. At first, Angel was surprised to realize how much thought he had put into each one beforehand. Then, she saw that it was all a part of Dylan's makeup, of his giving careful thought to everything he did. And while sometimes he came up with the wrong answer or an invention that didn't go anywhere, he learned from each experience. That was a lesson for her.

When Clifton finally left, after she had Audrette had cleaned up their mess and were falling into bed, their eyes barely open, she realized that she had played putt-putt and eaten Dylan's electric hot dogs while wearing her pink rose corsage.

Somehow, it seemed very appropriate for the festive evening.

─NINETEEN─

CHANGES

Angel glanced from the boxes on the front porch to the road, cupping her hand over her eyes to shade them from the blinding morning sun. The wide swath of dirt road was just as empty as five minutes before.

Loading her stuff into her father's car would take only a few more minutes, and if she knew her father, he'd want to leave right away. He had to get ready for a trial.

Angel opened one of the sealed boxes and began taking things out of it.

"What are you doing?" Gary demanded as he emerged from the house with a box. His face was red and he was frowning. "We'll never finish this if you unpack what you've already packed. We need to get on the road."

"All right." Angel sighed as she returned her shoes and other clothes to the box. She knew she was being foolish — Audrette had passed up a dozen opportunities to come by in the last few weeks. She was reminded of the day she moved to Crookwood, when Cat was supposed to come to her house and didn't.

Dylan came out on the porch, slamming the screen door behind him. He wore swim trunks and a T-shirt and was waiting for Gaylon to get home from work and take him to visit his new friend Jeremy, who had moved into a nearby house on the river. They went swimming every day. Dylan's deep brown tan made Angel envious.

"How much are you going to miss me, Dill? Think you can stand it?"

"Miss you? Yeah, I'll miss you lots — when I don't have to wait around to use the bathroom, when I can watch what I want on television, when Mom makes my favorite foods — you bet. I'll miss you like a toothache."

"So, what'll be different?" Angel tossed a tennis shoe at him. It hit his thigh. He grabbed it and stuffed it into the waistband of his trunks. "I think I'll keep this to remember you by."

Angel shrugged. "Go ahead. I don't know why I packed those shoes anyway. It's too hot to wear shoes in the summer. I'm going to wear sandals all summer."

"Does that include all your dates with Cliffie?"

Angel blushed. She had been out with Clifton Neal three times since the dance where they didn't dance — once for a hamburger and the movies, and twice to go swimming. She guessed they would see each other more when she moved in with her father, since Cliff lived in town too.

"Angelsea has a boyfriend, Angelsea has a boyfriend," sang Dylan, prancing around the porch with the tennis shoe on his head.

Angel picked up the other shoe. "I'm aiming for your mouth this time," she threatened.

"Why are you throwing perfectly good shoes at your brother?" asked a voice behind her.

Angel turned, grinning. Audrette was wearing yellow shorts, a white T-shirt and tennis shoes. Her hair was loose around her face.

"I'd throw your old boots if I had 'em. Now that would make an impression on him." Dylan made a face and ran inside.

"Fine way to treat a friend," Audrette sniffed, sitting down on the top porch step, her back to Angel.

"So we're still friends?"

"You tell me." Audrette had a piece of straw in her mouth and she stared into the distance. Then she turned around and looked at Angel. "You're the one who's moving. Not me."

"Just because I'm moving doesn't mean I don't want to be friends. I would have been glad to explain that to you, if you hadn't walked away when I told you."

"Would you explain it now?"

Angel sighed. "I got a job, Audrette. At Martha's Green Thumb — they were impressed with all the plant stuff I knew how to do."

"What you learned from me and Gram," sniffed Audrette.

"That's right, and from my mom. You could have gotten the job instead of me, if you had been interested. Anyway, there's no way I could have taken the job living out here. I don't have a car, remember? And my father has a two-bedroom apartment."

"You could have gone in with your mother. She's still working, isn't she?"

"Yes, but how would I get home? My job is full time for the summer, and hers isn't. Besides, we wouldn't be working the same days. If there was any other way, Audrette, I'd do it."

Audrette turned around and stared at Angel. "There is another way. You don't have to take the job. Then you could stay out here. I should never have introduced you to Cliff. I haven't seen you since you two met."

"And whose fault is that? I've called you about fifteen times! And I already told you, I'd rather not move — Clifton or not."

"Then why do it?" Audrette yelled.

"Because we need the money!" Angel yelled back, wanting to shake Audrette's skinny shoulders until her teeth rattled.

Audrette pressed her lips together in a thin, angry line. There was a long silence.

After a moment, Angel plopped down beside her friend.

"I'm sorry I yelled. Look, Mom is buying this house. She needs to save every cent she can, and not having to buy stuff for me will help. Besides, you know how hard getting a summer job is when you're our age. Everybody's out there looking, and no one wants to hire a kid. I couldn't say no. As much as I want to stay out here."

"So," Audrette looked at her sideways, "you're sure you're coming back?"

"Of course. I told you — Mom's buying the house. Where else would I live?"

"With your father?"

Angel shook her head. "Nope. This is home. Besides, there's a good chance Dad might move in. Anything could happen."

"That's good, I guess," said Audrette.

Angel's mother drove up, and Gary went out to meet her car. Angel and Audrette watched them hug each other.

Audrette made a face, which Angel ignored. They might look sappy to others, but Angel would rather see them hug in public than fight in private.

"You're the only friend I've ever had," muttered Audrette.

"Same goes for me, too. The only real friend."

Audrette turned red and jumped up. "I've got to go. I promised Gram I wouldn't be gone long." She shoved a paper bag into Angel's lap. "Don't open that until I'm gone, please."

"Wait a minute," said Angel. She stood up, went to the corner of the porch, and returned with a bougainvillea covered with large pink blooms.

"Here. This is my favorite plant. I thought it was dead last winter and was about to toss it when we moved out here. Dad rescued it and just brought it back today. He said he didn't do anything to it — it just came back on its own. I think it's kind of magic."

"Are you sure?"

Angel nodded. "Put it in the sun, don't water it much, and feed it a couple of times a month during the summer. Oh, don't pay any attention to me. You and Romie know what to do."

Audrette's eyes were bright. She lifted her hand in a quick wave and was gone. A few minutes later, when Angel couldn't stand the curiousity any longer, she sat down on the porch step, opened the paper bag and pulled out two of Romie's corn husk dolls, their arms linked. The shorter of the two wore glasses and had long hair. The tall one had short hair. A folded piece of paper was pinned to her skirt. Angel unpinned the paper and spread it out on her knees. The handwriting was Audrette's.

*"Dear Angelsea: Gram calls these bumpkins.
Please keep them with you so you won't forget
your roots in Crookwood. Love, Audrette."*

Angel laughed out loud. They had both given each other roots. She looked in the distance and squinted. Audrette was tiny, but Angel could see her as she waved with both arms. The plant was balanced atop her head. Angel stood up and returned the wave.

"What are you doing?" asked her father.

"Waving at Audrette. See her?"

He squinted in the direction Angel was pointing, but shook his head. "There's no one out there," he said.

Angel smiled. "I used to think that, too."

THE END

ABOUT THE AUTHOR

Barbara Elmore lives in Waco, Texas, where she is the managing editor of the Waco Tribune-Herald.